Back
on the
Streets

by

Deborah A. Ross

All rights reserved. This book is protected under the copyright laws of the United States of America. No part of this publication may be reproduced, stored in a retrieval system, or transmitted in any form or by any means—electronic, mechanical, photocopy, recording, or any other—except for brief quotations in printed reviews, without the prior written permission of the author.

Scripture quotations taken from the Holy Bible, New International Version. NIV Copyright © 1973, 1978, 1984 by International Bible Society. Used by permission of Zondervan Publishing House. All rights reserved.

Published by—
    3CrossPublishing
    9757 Widmer Road
    Lenexa, KS 66215
    www.3crosspublishing.com

Copyright © 2004 Deborah A. Ross
ISBN: 0-9754897-7-1

Contents

Dedication 4

Acknowledgements 6

Preface 9

Foreword 10

Introduction 13

Chapter One   Born Into Pain 15

Chapter Two   Abandoned 20

Chapter Three   Responsible for the Family 32

Chapter Four   My Downward Spiral 55

Chapter Five   A New Start 70

Chapter Six   The Healing Begins 94

Chapter Seven   Remarried 105

Chapter Eight   On the Streets Again 120

Chapter Nine   He Has a Plan for You Too 130

Chapter Ten   Stories for His Glory 138

Photo Gallery 165

Contact Information 175

Dedication

I dedicate this book to Maurice, my husband, friend, lover, and ministry partner. You are a gift from God. I love you greatly. Thank you for being a man of God. Thank you for loving me and not being ashamed of my past. Thank you for loving Ricky's children as your own and never treating them any differently than the three that came from our own union. You are a great dad. Without your love and support, there would be no JohnRoss Ministries. Thank you for having the sensitivity to combine your last name with Ricky's last name to form John(son)Ross Ministries, a name that would include all the children.

I also dedicate this book in memory of my first husband, Ricky Johnson. Thank you for entering my struggle and helping me to take care of my siblings.

DEDICATION

Thank you for taking such good care of me and making me feel so loved and so special. I look forward to seeing you in heaven.

Acknowledgements

To my Lord and Savior, Jesus Christ, I thank you for giving me a new life.

To my husband, friend and lover, Maurice, I love and appreciate you more than words can express. You are a gift to me and to the body of Christ. Thank you for supporting the vision that the Lord has placed in me. Thank you for not complaining about the house and meals as I sacrificed many hours writing this book.

To my children, I love you. Thank you for joining God's work. My prayer is that the next generation will take this ministry to the next level.

To my only and favorite, handsome, and gifted son, Ricky, God so loved the world that he gave his only son to die for the sins of the world. I so love people, but I can't imagine giving my only son to die for the sins of people. But I *can* imagine giving you Jesus, and that is what I have done.

To my eldest daughter, Rickena, God has gifted you to teach. Always use this gift to bring God glory. Please remember that whatever God begins, He is able to finish.

To my daughter, Sharice, God has allowed you to experience many miracles in your life. Continue to look

ACKNOWLEDGEMENTS

for the hand of God in your life, because you ain't seen *nothing* yet.

To my daughter, Monique, although God has blessed you to play all of your instruments well, there is an incredible anointing on your voice when you sing worship songs. Thank you for blessing me with your singing early in the morning. God has used you to bring me into His presence.

To my baby girl, Chaunte, you know the voice of God. He has revealed His will to you. You know the plans that He has for you. Don't stray to the left. The safest place is in the will of God. You will do greater works.

To my close and dear friend, Desiree Hoard, our relationship is a divine connection to accomplish His purposes. Thank you for being a faithful friend, committed Board member and loyal armor bearer. Thanks for stepping up to the call of leadership on the "Woman to Woman" committee. Your leadership has allowed me the time I needed to finish this book. I am sure our heavenly Father is looking at you and saying, "Well done, good and faithful servant."

To my friend, Lisa Buethe, God used you to renew my faith that this book could and should be written. Thank you for the countless hours that you spent helping me. Thank you for believing in the book and in me.

To my contributing editor and new friend, Kimmarie Rosa, God has given you so many gifts and talents. Thank you for the time and energy you have put into this book. You are precious. I consider it a real privilege to have worked with such a gifted woman. I anticipate great things ahead for you.

To our Board members and friends, Tommy and Desiree Hoard, Mark and Judy Raether and Dallas and Linda Strom, I thank all of you for faithfully serving as Board members and believing in street ministry.

To Lorraine Burroughs, thank you for embracing me as your daughter in the faith and allowing my children to call you "Grandma."

To the Volunteer Missionaries who work with the street ministry, thank you all for your labor of love.

Preface

The purpose of this book is to give hope to the hopeless. Many of us have been faced with trials that overwhelm us to the point of being unable to see our way out, and in despair we give up.

Then there are those people who may look at the "hopeless" and determine that there is, indeed, no way out for them, and they give up on these people as well. They invest no time, no energy, and no belief that the "hopeless" will ever make it. They give up on us before ever giving us a chance.

I trust that after reading this book, you will be encouraged whether you are feeling hopeless or are dealing with those who are "hopeless." There is hope for the "hopeless."

Foreword

Women who insist on changing their world are hard to find these days, but we find one here! Reading Deborah's book and knowing a little about her ministry in our city of Milwaukee touched me at a deep point. "Who shall I send and who will go for me" cried The Almighty in Isaiah chapter 6. "Here am I send me" replied Isaiah. God then promised to send him to the spiritually blind, deaf and hard hearted! Isaiah didn't change his mind but was obedient to the heavenly vision. He went because he was sent. It wasn't easy but it was necessary.

After the same manner this couple has trusted in the One who sits on the throne, and have obeyed His call. Their work and testimony will challenge our easy lives, but also bring a deep reminder that the call of God to sacrificial service pertains to all of us. Our sorry world needs Jesus.

Jill Briscoe
Internationally acclaimed speaker, ministry mentor, life coach and author of more than 40 books

Deborah Ross has a story to tell. It is one of God's activity in the midst of pain and abuse. In her book Back to the Streets *she has journeyed into her childhood to offer hope and healing to other wounded women and present them with the offer of grace. Grace transformed Deborah into a woman of courage, hope and love. God's love sent her back to the street. Deb-*

FOREWORD

orah has a passion to cooperate with God to spread this Good, Glad News to other desperate hearts. The story is told in this book.

Linda Strom
Author of *Karla Faye Tucker/Set Free*
Co-founder of Discipleship Unlimited

Introduction

As I stepped off the stage and onto the vacant lot littered with broken glass, all sorts of trash, and the ever-present weeds, a girl about nine or ten years old worked her way out of the crowd and walked towards me. Her clothes were mismatched and dirty. Her hair was uncombed. She carried with her the grime and smell of a hard city life. Yet, beneath the rough exterior I saw a pretty young girl whose eyes gave away her pain and hopelessness. Softly she said to me, "I listened to everything you said, and my life is just like yours was."

I was caught off guard. Not because she was emotional, quite the contrary. She spoke quietly in a matter-of-fact tone, and for a few seconds I was disconnected

INTRODUCTION

from her. It was as though I were looking into a mirror. My vision was blurred from the tears that filled my eyes. Warm tears began to run down my cheeks. The floodgate was open, I couldn't stop crying. The years of my own neglect and abuse flashed through my mind. I had just shared a story of my past life, a life that I had lived over twenty years ago, but standing before me now was this child, living with the same struggles and pain I had endured in my past, only she was living them *today*. The reality of her situation was all too familiar to me, and my heart began to ache. At first, all I could think to do was to pray silently, "Dear God, why do innocent children have to suffer so much?"

She waited patiently, not saying a word, but her dark eyes were watching me as I gathered my thoughts and began to talk to her. I asked her if she had prayed with me just moments before. She responded with a yes. I assured her that even though she did not understand why her life was the way it was now, God understood and had a plan for her. I encouraged her to talk to God every day. I told her that even though she may feel alone, God is always present and will never abandon her. He would be there for her and He would give her a new life, just as He had done for me. Later, as we began to pack to leave, I couldn't stop thinking about the girl and my own life, and how far God had brought me to where I was today.

Chapter One

Born Into Pain

I was born in the sixties. Doctors would now label me as a Fetal Alcohol Syndrome baby, but we didn't have that term then. My mother consumed a great deal of alcohol during her pregnancy with me and with all the siblings that came after me. As adults, my brothers and sisters would sometimes tease each other about who had which symptoms of FAS. Over the years I have tried to understand what went wrong with Mom and why she lived in the bottle. No one has been able to provide any concrete answers, least of all Mom herself.

It all began in 1940 when my mother, Alma Jean Murphy, was born. Just six years later, her mother died and left little Alma without a family. As a young girl, I didn't give much thought to how devastating it must have been for Mom to lose her mother at such a young age. Two possible daddies, both of them married, quietly claimed her but took no responsibility for raising or supporting her. With no brothers or sisters, my mother would have been very alone if it hadn't been for my grandmother's best friend. Her name was Alma too, but we all called her Auntie. She was a beautiful woman with long, jet black, wavy hair.

Auntie was hardworking, energetic and an excellent housekeeper. She was a faithful member of Sunrise Missionary Church in Memphis, Tennessee, and held high values and moral standards. Although my mother was an orphan, she was not left penniless. My grandmother, upon her death, had left my mom a decent amount of money and several properties from her estate. So, despite her early misfortune and suffering, one could say that my mother had a fairly good start at a new life. She had much training in the fine arts. She had learned to sing opera and tap dance, and played several instruments including the piano, organ, piccolo and flute. Whenever my mother's friends would tell of their experiences working in the cotton fields, my mother would boast that her feet had never stepped into a cotton field. She also boasted that Auntie wouldn't allow her to spend too much time in the sun for fear of heat stroke. Auntie had done the best she could to give my mother a quality life.

My mother married at just sixteen years of age. Auntie had approved of the marriage to my dad, Lorenzo White. He was twenty years old and a hard-working, decent man. Before long they had two daughters, Pam and Gale. I have no memories of my dad ever living with us. My two older sisters have those precious memories. I am the third child born to them. They had separated before I was old enough to realize that there had even been a union.

BACK ON THE STREETS

I would dream about my mom and dad getting back together. I would wonder what life would be like to have my dad and mom living in the same house. I wanted a normal home and the security that came with it.

I would ask my mother, "Mom, why doesn't Dad live with us?"

She would bitterly reply, "Because he loved another woman more than he loved us. He just didn't love us enough to stay."

I couldn't get over that. I had so many questions. My dad didn't love me enough to stay with me? He loved another woman more than he loved his own children? How could that have happened? How could he just reject us and walk away like that? Doesn't he know how we feel? Doesn't he care? My dad, however, had different answers to the same questions. He said, "I tried to live with your mom, but I just couldn't handle her drinking problem."

More questions followed. My mother's drinking drove my daddy away? Why does she do this to us? Why doesn't she fix it? After hearing my dad's version of the story, I was very angry with my mom.

I began to think that if I could get her to stop drinking, then my dad would come back home. I hunted down her hidden bottles and poured them out. I pleaded with her and told her I didn't like what she did and who she became when she drank. I spent my entire childhood, and even some adult years, trying to get Mom to stop drinking. Eventually I would learn that there was nothing that I could do to stop my mom from drinking. It was a long, hard road to travel for all of us.

Chapter Two

Abandoned

When I was about two and a half years old, my little sister Rena and I were living with our mom. My two older sisters were living in Memphis with Auntie. At that time we lived on the first level of an old, three-story apartment building. I paced back and forth over the worn, hardwood floors. The boards were complaining with creaks and moans, so I froze and looked nervously over to where my sister had finally collapsed and was sleeping. She had worn herself out crying. At least she was finally quiet. She was nestled in the sunken cushion of our old, worn couch. Her nose was so stuffy that she was breathing through her mouth, which made a little "O" between her tearstained cheeks. I didn't want to risk waking her again, so I sat down right where I was and leaned up against the wall. Where was Mom?

I don't know how long I had been sleeping, but Rena woke me with sobbing wails. I ran to the front door, brushed away the torn plastic curtain, and looked through the wood-trimmed glass door. Then I ran to the bedroom and thought I saw Mom lying under the covers of the bed, so I called to her and tugged on the blanket, "Come, Mama! Rena cry! Mama!"

The sheets unraveled to reveal an empty bed. I stood there a minute trying to figure out where she was. I ran back to Rena and picked up a bottle from the floor. I tried shoving the sticky, dirty nipple in her mouth just to stop the screaming, but Rena wouldn't take it. She only screamed more loudly, and her little body was ridged with indignation. I didn't know what to do.

BACK ON THE STREETS

My father eventually found us when he came for his weekly visit. He took us home to live with him and his girlfriend. She did not have children of her own at that time, so while my dad worked, she took care of my sister and me. No one knows for sure how long we had been left alone. Dad believed it had been at least a couple of days, because Rena was soaked in urine and had had several bowel movements. Her bottom was raw and bloody from the soiled diaper.

With my older sisters living with Auntie in Memphis, Tennessee, and Rena and me living with my dad, Mom could really enjoy her freedom. That freedom and party life got her to her fifth pregnancy. After giving birth to my brother Kenny, Mom decided to gather all of her children and bring us to live with her and her new live-in boyfriend. Mom had a knack for attracting the worst kind of men. They were unemployed, alcoholics and abusive. She feared being alone and always had a man living with her. Consequently, more children were born. My brothers Tony and Charles and my baby sister, Jean, were all added to the family. Before long we could see that the older children had been brought back to take care of the little ones.

In the earlier years, most of the responsibility was placed on my two older sisters, Pam and Gale. They resented taking care of Mom's children. In Auntie's comfortable, stable home, they could still be children themselves. When they were with Mom, their responsibilities became those of adults.

They were responsible for cleaning the house, as well as for bathing, dressing, feeding and tending to all the needs that young children have, while being only seven and eight years old themselves. Their resentment sometimes made them harsh towards us. They knew their childhoods were being taken away from them. The rest of us would *never* know a normal childhood.

BACK ON THE STREETS

Most every morning, Mom would leave the house to hang out with her friends. She would tell us to stay in the apartment, and would often be gone all day and well into the night. We would have to amuse ourselves, so whenever Mom left, we would have "searches." We weren't looking for anything in particular, but one day we found something fascinating in a dresser drawer. It was a shiny thirty-five millimeter bullet. We were playing cowboys and Indians when one of us came up with the idea to put the bullet in a can and light a match to it. We all crowded around with great anticipation to see what would happen.

It wasn't long before there was a loud explosion and my sister Gale yelled, "I've been shot!" The bullet had grazed her arm and blood was streaming from the wound. My sister Pam, now a Registered Nurse, immediately took charge and sent me to get a Band-Aid and peroxide from the neighbors downstairs so that she could treat the wound. I ran as fast as my heart was beating, wondering whether my sister was going to die! Of course, with just a flesh wound to her arm, Gale survived, but still has a significant scar to this day. We never told Mom what happened.

Another day, on a warm, summer afternoon, we were tired of staying in the apartment. It was nice out, so we decided to play on the narrow wooden second-floor porch. The children from down the street saw us and started yelling and throwing rocks. They had a whole alley full of "ammunition," but we didn't have anything to throw back other than the rocks that had landed on the porch. Obviously they were winning, so we ran into the house and slammed the door. My brother Tony was a crawling baby at that time and was sitting on the kitchen floor. Just then a rock flew through the kitchen window and the glass shattered into his face. Blood was everywhere. Tony was screaming, and the cut under his eye was so deep that he had to have stitches.

All eight of Mom's children carry the physical scars of our unsupervised childhoods. Most of the time, Mom was unaware of what caused those scars. We weren't bad children. We just weren't trained and properly cared for. Of course, our bodies would heal over time, but it was the emotional scars that took so much longer to heal.

Although we were frequently left alone, the nighttime was the scariest. Noises came alive at night, and so did our imaginations. We laugh about it now, but there was a particular time that we all remember well. We were playing when my sister thought she saw a stranger in the living room. One by one, we all peeked around the corner and convinced ourselves that there really was a stranger sitting in the living room. In a panic we ran for the pantry, crammed ourselves inside and silently closed the door. Pam, the oldest and bravest at that moment, decided that if we were going to be attacked, we should attempt to die in the order of our age. We obediently lined up with the oldest siblings closest to the door. I was the third in line to die. Every time we dared to peek into the living room, we would see the stranger. We stayed that way for hours. We all were getting very hungry, but there was nothing to eat in the pantry but a bottle of syrup and an old can of shortening. Finally our mother came home and we ran out to discover that the "person" we had seen was really a combination of shadows and not an attacker after all. Our imaginations had gotten the better of us. Sadly, the reality of what was to come was far more horrifying than anything we could have imagined for ourselves.

    Mom tried to be a disciplinarian, but she was abusive. When she was drinking, she was irritable. When she didn't have her booze, she was even more irritable.

She had never learned how and when to apply physical discipline. One night I was awakened to my mom standing over me with a bottle she had broken. Her arm was raised and she was holding it as though she were about to stab me. Rena was next to me, so I grabbed her, pushed my mother down, and we ran out of the apartment. When we came back with the neighbors, Mom was knocked out drunk. When the neighbor was able to wake her, he asked her, "Jean, why are you trying to hurt the children?" Mom responded, "What are you talking about?" She did not remember what had happened.

More often, we were beaten with an extension cord until our skin broke open, and then Mom would pour alcohol on the open wound. Another night, at about two o'clock in the morning, I was shocked out of a deep sleep by an extension cord slashing across my back. I began screaming, "What are you doing? What did I do?!"

In a low, even voice, she said only, "You know what you did," and she continued beating me.

I wanted her to stop, so I started guessing. "Was it my day for dishes?"

She grumbled, "No," and continued to beat me.

I kept trying to guess and she only kept saying "No" until finally she came up with an answer, "You didn't sweep the floor good enough and you left trash under the table. Now get up and sweep!"

There was nothing to do but get up and sweep, so I did.

An absentee father and a drunken mother left us unprotected from all kinds of abuse.

My very first memory of being molested is when I was three years old. That event is too dark to write about, but countless times were to follow. I remember one night, waking from a deep sleep; I could feel a presence over me. I'm not sure why I opened my eyes, but when I did there was a naked man standing over me. I froze. He was just standing there, watching me. When he saw that I was awake, he came towards me. Mom was knocked out drunk in the next room and everyone else was asleep. He began to climb into my bed. I was terrified and tried to hold him away from me. I remember the strength of his arms, but I fought hard to keep him off of me. Afraid that I would wake everyone up, he finally stopped and turned to leave the room. As he walked away he hissed at me, "You're a slut and a whore!"

I knew he would try again another time and I was right.

There were many other times when men were successful in violating me sexually. Eventually I got up the nerve to tell my mom what her boyfriends were doing to me, but she didn't believe me. It didn't matter what I said they did or how many times they did it. She would just look me in the eye and say, "You are a liar."

I quickly learned to stop telling, because there was no reason to. No one would believe me anyway.

Chapter Three

Responsible for the Family

My mother's alcoholism was a real nightmare. Her drinking progressed as the years passed, and our quality of life continually deteriorated. Although Mom drank during my entire childhood, in the earlier years she cooked and cleaned more often and had more sober days than drunken days. Boyfriends came and went. Some of them lived with us for periods of time and all of them encouraged my mother's drinking. One particular boyfriend was with us for a rather long time. Being a "functioning alcoholic," he kept his drinking primarily to the weekends, but by this time my mother was drinking daily. When he got home from work, he wanted to see a tidy house and a meal prepared. By now my mother rarely cooked or cleaned, and the physical abuse began. He would demand, "Jean, why is the house like this? Been drinking again, haven't you?"

She would lie and slur the words, "I have not had a drink all day!"

Then the sound of fists pounding on my mother would fill the room. I was awakened many nights by screaming and fighting. Nothing, not even our little fingers in our ears, could stop the sound of hits and punches to our mother's face and body. It often sounded so violent that I was sure he would kill her. If we dared to try to stop the beating, the boyfriend would turn on us with swearing and threats. We were ordered from the room only to huddle together and cry until it was over. The next day her face would be so disfigured by the swelling, bruises and cuts that she didn't look human. I remember many times believing her face would never return to normal again. Sometimes I would hear her talking on the phone with her girlfriends and she would say, "I brought this on myself. He wouldn't beat me if he didn't love me." I decided as a young girl that I never wanted that type of love.

I created a mission for myself. I was going to get my mother to stop drinking. I would search all over the house for her stashed bottles and whenever I found one, I would pour its contents down the sink. One day she caught me and tried to stop me from emptying the bottle completely. "What in the **** are you doing?" She yelled and moved towards me.

I didn't answer her, but started shaking the bottle hoping it would drain faster.

"Give me that!" she snarled, and made another grab for the bottle.

I pulled the bottle out of her reach and tried to hold her off with my other arm. Some of the alcohol splashed across my face as I struggled to empty the rest of it into the drain. I could feel how cold it was as it evaporated on my skin. I shivered. The bottle was almost empty when Mom made one last desperate attempt to snatch it away. Infuriated, she grabbed my arm instead and dug her fingernails into my skin, leaving me with deep, bloody gouges on my arm. The bottle was finally empty, so she shoved me away.

"I don't believe in abortions," she yelled, "but I should have killed you when I had the chance, you lowdown child!"

I stood there, shocked at her words, but I wanted her to try to understand. I said, "Mom, I'm trying to help you to stop drinking!"

"Kiss my ***!" was her answer, and she stormed out to get another bottle.

She left me standing there with a bleeding arm, a broken heart, and a tough resolve to be sneakier when pouring out her alcohol in the future.

One day a friend told me that she had seen my mother drunk, wandering in the middle of the street and was almost hit by a car. I began to fear for her life, and was afraid to let her leave the house that evening. She was still drunk, preparing to go out again to get more alcohol. I wanted her to stay home.

"Hey, Mom, how about we play some cards?" I said, trying to make my voice sound casual.

"I don't want to play any cards." She mumbled while getting her purse ready.

"Come on, Mom. We can play monopoly, or jacks. We'll just spend some time together. How does that sound?"

She was making her way toward the door. I stepped in front of her. "Girl, get out the way…" she ordered.

I stood my ground. "No. I don't want you to go out tonight."

"Move out of my way, Deborah Ann." She stumbled, trying to get around me. I held my arms out, blocking the door, but when she saw how serious I was, she became even more determined. We struggled with each other for a while. She fought back hard, cussing the whole time, but I had come this far. I wasn't going to back down now. Finally she got tired and simply collapsed on the floor and wouldn't look at me. I got down on the floor too, and leaned up against the door so no one could go in or out.

The next morning, we awoke and found ourselves in the same place. Mom couldn't remember why we were there. She was completely unaware of what had happened the night before. She remembered nothing. I didn't care. I felt relieved. I believed that I had saved her life that night. I had succeeded, and I had to take my victories wherever I could get them.

School was a place where I could succeed much of the time. I loved school. School meant not only that I was away from home, but also that I could eat. Before the free lunch program was in the public schools, we had off-campus lunches. Many children went home for lunch. I just went home. Eventually, I was one of the children who benefited from the government's free meal programs that were available later. I can remember watching the clock, longing for the lunch bell to ring so that I could put something in my tummy. I did not want to miss school, because that meant I would miss getting to eat that day.

I was a good student and I loved to learn. I was a straight-A student, which on the one hand was great. On the other hand, it was just another reason for the school kids to target me and give me a hard time. I was frequently at the mercy of bullies who made me do their homework for them. This continued until the sixth grade, when I decided that I had had enough.

I was walking out from the cafeteria during our lunch break. I was already feeling angry because Beverly, the toughest girl in the class, had taken more than half my lunch. I was hungry. There hadn't been much to eat at home that week, and I had been looking forward to my lunch. As I was standing on the playground, trying to decide what to do, I heard Beverly laugh and say, "Don't get too close. She stinks, you know. You might pass out from the smell."

I didn't have to turn around to know whom she was talking about. It was hard to keep myself and my clothes clean. Most of the time we didn't have basic toiletries or cleaning products. I had one or two pair of panties at the time, which I washed out in the bathroom sink when we did have soap or laundry detergent. I sighed, and then turned around to face her. Some of the other kids were laughing too.

"No wonder she stinks." Beverly continued. "I bet she hasn't had a bath in a month."

That did it. My ears were buzzing with the blood rushing to them. I was tired, I was hungry, I didn't need to be humiliated too.

The other students gasped as I aggressively moved toward her. Before I knew what I was doing, I let loose all the years of rage on her. I had had enough. I punched, scratched, clawed and screamed. By the time it was over, I had beaten the toughest girl in the school, and that was the last time anyone ever messed with me.

Outside of the recess drama, I really liked school and dreaded when it was time to go home. As I got closer to our apartment, I would feel a heavy weight of depression press down on me. We were never sure what condition we would find our mother in. From sober to sloppy drunk were all possibilities on any day of the week. Whoever reached home first would give the report to the rest of us as we arrived. We needed to be prepared for what we had to deal with that day.

We had code words to describe Mom's condition. Sober meant that she had nothing to drink. If the report was that Mom was "tipsy," it meant that she had been drinking but was still functioning somewhat normally. "High" meant that she had quite a bit to drink, her speech was slurred, and she staggered as she walked. "Drunk" meant that she could not stand without falling. "Sloppy drunk," the worst of all, meant that she was knocked out cold, couldn't be awakened, and probably was lying in her own vomit or urine. Because of the good chance that we would find Mom in this last condition, we rarely ever brought anyone home with us. Home was a hard place to be because we were so often embarrassed or ashamed.

BACK ON THE STREETS

When I was about eleven years old, my two older sisters were sent to live with our dad. Now all the responsibility of taking care of the children and running the house became mine. We were close in age, but the younger ones looked to me to meet their needs. Whenever they were hungry, they would come and tell me. I was the one they asked for permission to go outside. Our living conditions were terrible. The stench was strong, and the house was always cluttered and filthy. Rats and roaches skittered everywhere. We didn't even react to them because we were so used to living with them.

We were raised on welfare. Every month Mom would get food stamps and money. She would use the cash to buy alcohol and sell the stamps to buy more alcohol. Bills were left unpaid. We often had no groceries in the house. Both the gas and electricity were rarely on at the same time. When the electricity was off, we sat in the dark or used candles for light. When the gas was turned off, we used a hot plate to cook food for our meals and heat water to wash with. Sometimes we were so hungry that we were physically weak and could manage only to sleep and awaken. We struggled to pay the rent, and were used to moving from place to place because of evictions.

Because we were always running out of food, we collected and sold pop bottles. Over time, I learned what foods to buy that would get us the furthest. We relied on flour, shortening, potatoes and onions to make French fries and onion rings. My brothers began to shoplift food when they could, and when the neighborhood gardens were ready, they would steal what they could out of them. A couple of times my brother even took steaks right off of backyard grills! I joined in by stealing from Mom. I would wait until she was knocked out drunk and then reach into her bosom, where she kept the money and food stamps. I was so tired of being hungry, sitting in the dark, and cooking on a hot plate. I took over paying the bills and doing the shopping. I was becoming the lady of the house at just eleven years old.

Although my father was not living with us, he was never entirely absent from our lives. He had a new family, two girls and a boy, and lived in the south suburbs of Chicago. He would buy a new Cadillac every year, and every Friday night, after working his second shift, he would drive his Cadillac out to see his children. We used to wait up for him, sitting in the window and watching for that shiny, clean Cadillac to pull up. We would sing our "Daddy" song: "Here come Daddy. Here come Daddy. Here come Daddy, Daddy, Daddy!!"

The warm summer months were the best, because everyone in the neighborhood would be outside and they would see my dad.

RESPONSIBLE FOR THE FAMILY

I was proud of my dad. His visit each Friday lasted only about ten minutes, but it was the highlight of my week. He was my favorite parent. He didn't drink like my mom and her boyfriends. He gave each of his children an allowance of two dollars a week. In the earlier years, he gave Mom money for food and half the amount of her rent. Then later, he stopped giving her money for rent and gave her only grocery money. After I complained that Mom would use the money only for alcohol and cigarettes, we worked out a routine. Some Fridays, not often but when he had enough time, he would take me to the twenty-four-hour grocery store and give me the same amount of money that he would have given to Mom. It was never enough to cover food for everyone for the whole week, and when I told him this, he replied, "It's not my responsibility to take care of all the children in that house. They are not all mine. Ask their dads for help."

The truth was that they were not all his children or his responsibility. They were mine.

I took the burden of caring for my siblings seriously. I took care of my family, handled all the household matters, and continued with school. Then came my special day when I was to graduate from the eighth grade! All the girls were talking about what they were going to wear and what they were going to do to celebrate. I didn't have anything nice to wear, but I hoped to have a new dress because Dad had promised to get me one. The day before graduation, I called him and said, "Dad, you said you were going to buy me a dress. Graduation is tomorrow and I don't have one yet."

He replied, "Are you calling me a liar?" Dad I don't have a dress. Dad then said "for calling me a liar you will not get a dress." I thought my dad would at least come to the ceremony, but there was no one in the audience for me. I fully expected my mother to be absent. I almost hoped she wouldn't come because of the condition I knew she would be in, but I really had hoped my dad would show up. The sharp pain of reality set in. My dad didn't love me. It struck me, how could he love me when he continued to allow me to live in the conditions I lived in? He had all of his needs met and I would go days without eating. He saw my dirty, raggedy clothes and did nothing about them. He was allowing all of this to happen, and I could only think that it was because he didn't love me. But, despite even this, I still loved him.

The school principal called my name, "Deborah White." I walked across the stage, in the only dress I had to wear, and accepted my diploma. As I walked back to my seat, I looked out over the crowd and felt more alone than I had ever remembered feeling. Hot tears burned in my eyes, but I refused to let them fall. I choked down the lumps rising in my throat and sat through the rest of the ceremony trying to distract myself from the loneliness. Afterwards, I saw all the families taking pictures, posing for group photos, laughing and talking about their plans. There were grandparents, parents, siblings, and even friends for everyone else. I felt an ache in my chest. Someone asked me what my plans were for the rest of the day. I lifted my chin and forced a bright smile, "Oh, my mom and dad both had to work, but they are taking me out for dinner and a movie later." Then I went home and cried myself to sleep.

I wanted my younger siblings to never experience that kind of pain. I wanted them to know that someone cared. At the very least, they should know that I cared. I made sure they had nice clothes to wear to their graduations, and I was always there to celebrate them and their accomplishments. Like a protective parent, I wanted better for them than what I had.

RESPONSIBLE FOR THE FAMILY

I decided that our holidays needed to be improved. Mom didn't cook holiday meals. Her idea of celebrating was to share her bottles with us. We would go to the liquor store with her and she would let us choose our drink, then she would let us consume as much as we wanted. I remember getting toys for only two Christmases. When we went back to school after Christmas break, everyone would tell the others what they had gotten under their tree. I was not going to be outdone, so I would come up with a long list of imaginary things I had received for Christmas too, but I couldn't imagine away the fact that my brothers and sisters also had nothing.

One year I bought some lights and stuck them to the wall in the shape of a Christmas tree. I managed to get a few toys for the children, and wrapped them in newspaper to sit under our "wall-tree." I was pleased when I heard the "Oohs" and "Ahhs" coming from the children as they saw our Christmas decorations and gifts. They were so excited over a few inexpensive toys. It didn't take much to make that year a Christmas to remember.

I was fourteen when my boyfriend, Ricky, came to live with us. I can't recall when we first met, but we had known each other since we were small children. He came from a home where his parents worked hard to provide for their children. Although he came from a fairly decent home, Ricky was in a gang. Mom didn't seem to mind his hanging around. She was rarely home anymore anyway. He started spending a night here and there, and then eventually he just stayed. I was the woman of the house and he was the man of the house. Although Ricky had a decent home to go back to, he chose to enter our struggle.

One fall day, Rena and I got home from school at about the same time. We found the fire department there, putting out a blaze in our third-floor apartment.

As usual, Mom wasn't around. Only part of the kitchen had been burned, so we were told that the apartment was still in livable condition. The firefighters left, and Rena and I stood there in the apartment that we hated. It was filthy, run-down and infested. Now it had fire and smoke damage besides. Rena and I looked at each other and I came up with a plan. I had the idea that if the apartment were completely destroyed, we would have to go live with my dad. Rena agreed, so together we set fire to the kitchen and the bedrooms and then ran downstairs to watch the fire burn down our apartment. Before long, the fire truck returned again to a real blaze, and this time there was serious damage. My plan had worked!

I ran to the pay phone down the street and called my dad. I told him that there had been a fire, we had lost everything, and there was no place for us to go.

There was nothing else to do but for him to take Rena and me in. My brothers went to live with their dad, and Ricky went back to his parents.

I missed Ricky terribly. He had moved in when I was fourteen, and we had already been together for two years. While I was living with Dad, Ricky and I continued our relationship. We talked on the phone daily, and I saw him whenever I went to visit Mom. We would spend the night together whenever we had the chance.

My life was very different in the suburbs. We had a nice, clean house, and there were no rats or bugs. We were enrolled in school. I never had to worry about what I was going to eat, and I wore decent clothes. I was finally living with my dad. I thought that now he could really get to know me and love me. I was hopeful and happy, but Dad's girlfriend didn't share my excitement. Although she was not actually abusive to us, it was obvious that she did not want us there.

RESPONSIBLE FOR THE FAMILY

One day when she knew I was nearby, I overheard her telling someone on the phone that my dad wasn't really my dad. I felt confused and began to worry. Did my dad believe that I was not his child? I was convinced that I was his child because people always said that I was the spitting image of him. In fact, I resembled him more than his other children in his house. Not knowing what else to do and feeling quite desperate, I took an overdose of pills. Rena found me and when she realized what I had done, she ran for help. I was taken to the hospital to have my stomach pumped.

While I was there, I refused to speak to anyone until my dad came. When he arrived, he wanted to know why I had taken the pills. I told him that I had heard Tina say he wasn't my real daddy. He looked in my eyes and assured me that I was his child. I could hear him fussing at Tina later that night at home. He was very angry, and I was glad. But most of all, I was glad that he had told me I was his child. I needed to know that I was his child.

Chapter Four

My Downward Spiral

One day, as we were sitting down to dinner at my dad's house, the phone rang. It was my brother. He said, "Deborah, we don't have any food in the house. Mom's gone all the time and we haven't eaten in days. We're so hungry."

I immediately lost my appetite. Just as I had come up with a plan to get my dad to take me in, I began thinking of a plan to go back to Mom's. I figured that if I were back at Moms' house, Dad would have to come and bring me money again and then I could use the money to help take care of the younger ones. Pam and Gale were at separate colleges out of state, and I knew that if I didn't help the other children, no one would. Spring Break was coming, so I told my dad that I wanted to spend a week with Mom. When the break was over and Dad came to pick me up, I told him that I was going to stay with Mom. He didn't try to convince me to come back home with him. It was probably a relief for him and his girlfriend. After all, they now had three children together. So I moved back into my mom's house with my brothers and sisters.

The worst of our living conditions was when we moved into a condemned building. Again our home was roach- and rat-infested. Late at night, while trying to fall asleep, we could hear the rats scrambling around in the walls. These were Chicago's super-size rats. They were afraid of nothing and no one. The downstairs neighbor's dog had dared to face off with one of them and had been badly torn up. It took that poor dog months to recover.

One day I had to take my brother to the emergency room while playing jacks on the floor, he reached into a hole in the floor and had been bitten by a rat. These rats were dangerous. Whenever we saw one out in the open we would stump our foot to scare them back into their holes. Unlike mice that would run fast they would take their time and slowly wobble back to their hole.

The cockroach situation was out of control as well. Whenever anyone opened a cupboard, dozens of them would drop to the countertop and skitter away. We could actually hear their little bodies hit the tile. I used to play a game with them. I would close my eyes and then open them quickly, fixing on one spot. My goal was to find a spot in the room that was roach free. I would look in a different spot each time I opened my eyes. I never won the game. The cockroaches were everywhere.

There was no gas in the condemned three-story building. We had moved in during the summer months, so heat wasn't a problem yet. We had electricity, so we could use our hot plate to cook meals and heat water to wash with, but we had no heat when the winter set in. It was so cold in the apartment that the toilet and all the water pipes froze. We had no running water. We would use the toilet at the tavern around the corner. Just down the street, we had a fire hydrant that constantly trickled water. We would fill our buckets and empty milk containers with water. We would heat water on a hot plate to produce steam, and then all huddle together in one large bedroom to keep warm. Leaving the steam-heated bedroom to go into any other part of the apartment was just like stepping outside. We could see our breath freeze.

Ricky had come back to live with us, and I was so happy to have him in my life because I felt safe when he was around. He was a tall young man at six foot three and two hundred ten pounds. He carried all the water we needed and made sure we had food. My father continued to visit us on Fridays. Ricky would always hide, out of respect for my dad. I would ask my dad to drive me to the fire hydrant to get water. He carried the water in his Cadillac. I was trying to increase his awareness of our situation, hoping that he would have pity on us and help us. He would give me a few dollars, climb back into his Cadillac, and drive away to his home in the suburbs, where his other three children were loved and well cared for. I continued to steal Mom's welfare checks and food stamps and life went on as it had before, but I was getting ready to make some changes.

I had a plan for getting us out of the condemned building. I had managed to save enough of the stolen money, so Ricky and I began searching for a new place. Day after day, we would walk the cold and windy streets of Chicago's west side, looking for an apartment. We were so young that no one wanted to rent to us. After being turned down time and again, we knocked on still another door. An elderly woman opened it. She looked at us expectantly and said, "Yes, how may I help you?"

Ricky and I looked at each other and I started to talk. "We're interested in the apartment that you have for rent."

Her eyes narrowed and she asked, "And how old are you?"

Without missing a beat, I replied, "I'm twenty and my fiancé is twenty-one." I made sure to keep eye contact with her, but I could see she didn't believe us. She gave a little sigh of exasperation and started to close the door. I was freezing, hungry and tired. We had been looking for a place for days. In desperation, I put my hand up to stop her from closing the door and pleaded, "Please, ma'am, the truth is…"

MY DOWNWARD SPIRAL

I told her that we were living in the condemned building on 18th and Homan, and shared with her my mom's drinking problem. By the time I was finished telling her my story, she was in tears and agreed to let us have the place. We had an understanding that the rent money would always come from me and not my mother. I promised to handle everything. I asked my dad to help us move. Surprisingly, he rented a truck and helped us, although we didn't have much furniture to move. While moving the sofa, my brother found a litter of baby rats in it, which we had to kick out before moving the sofa.

Our new place was much smaller. It was a two-bedroom apartment with a living room and kitchen. Ricky and I had one bedroom and the children had the other bedroom. When Mom was around, she slept in the living room. The place was a little nicer than the condemned building. We now had heat and running water.

We still had a problem with rats and roaches, but by now that was a way of life for us.

At the age of sixteen, I was pregnant with my first child. I was determined to finish high school, and even attended an alternative school for pregnant girls to help with my credits. Ricky dropped out of school. He had decided that I was smarter, so I should stay in school and he would stay home and care for the baby. He took such good care of me during my pregnancy. Our apartment was on the third floor, so when I arrived home from school I would yell up to him and he would come bounding down the steps to carry me up three flights of stairs. He would fuss at me if I climbed the stairs. He didn't want me to risk having a miscarriage. He was very attentive to me. My friends told me how lucky I was to have a boyfriend like Ricky.

He took on the responsibilities of cooking and cleaning while I was pregnant. The home was always clean and dinner was ready when I came in from school. Ricky catered to all my cravings. It didn't matter how late it was or how much it cost. Ricky would make sure that I had it. Two months after my seventeenth birthday, I gave birth to our son. He weighed in at eight pounds five ounces, which was an excellent weight for the baby of a teenaged girl weighing only one hundred fifteen pounds to begin with. Ricky could not have been more proud. It had been his goal for me to have a big, healthy baby. I named our son Ricky Lorenzo after his dad and my dad.

Late one night, we awoke to knocking on the door. It was one of Ricky's hustling friends. He said to Ricky, "What's up, man? You want to make some easy money?"

Ricky didn't hesitate, and said, "Just give me a minute to get dressed."

When he came back to the room, I pleaded with him. "Ricky, I have a bad feeling about this one. Please don't go."

Ricky just grinned and waved me off. "You don't need to worry. I'll be back soon."

I wasn't about to give up, and was very aggressive about asking him to stay. I reminded him of our friends who had gotten caught and how we now had Little Ricky to think of. Big Ricky just smiled, gave me a kiss and said, "Baby, I'll see you later. Don't worry."

Ricky had hustled before. It's how we survived at the time. Ricky would steal out of grocery stores or from inside cars, or take hubcaps off. He stayed away from the more violent crimes and those that were person to person.

Ricky left the house with his friend and returned in less than an hour in handcuffs with the police. The friend had gotten away. Ricky was charged with theft and sentenced to three years in prison. He left me with a five-month-old baby to care for.

I couldn't finish high school now. There was no one to watch the baby. I dropped out as a senior, and my dreams of going to college were gone. I had thought I might become a lawyer. Meanwhile, Mom had moved a new boyfriend into the small apartment that Ricky and I had found. One day she came to me and said, "There's not enough room here for you and my man. One of you has got to go, and my man isn't going anywhere."

So, once again, I found myself looking for a home, but this time I was alone with a five-month-old baby. At first I moved in with some small-time drug dealers. Later I moved into another condemned building with two other teen moms. There I fell into a depression. I began to drink. At first I began drinking the same things I had seen my mother drink, such as whisky, vodka and gin. Then I decided that I didn't want to be like my mom, so I limited myself to wine coolers, beer, and pink champale.

I developed the habit of smoking cigarettes up to a pack-and-a-half a day. Then I started smoking marijuana, as well as smoking, snorting, and then eating cocaine and other drugs. I started hanging out in nightclubs. Survival was the name of the game. I met an older man and moved in with him. Although he took care of my son and me, I had no feelings for him or any of the other men that I was with during the time Ricky was in prison. They used me and I used them. They provided me with a roof over my head, a meal ticket and a constant supply of drugs. My brothers and sisters were on their own now too.

I visited Ricky once a month while he was in prison. He was four hours away, so Little Ricky and I would catch the Greyhound bus to visit him. On those weekends we stayed in a motel and saw Ricky at every visiting hour that was allowed. We also wrote many letters. He even proposed to me from behind bars, but soon called it off, saying that he didn't want prison to be a part of our wedding memories. I would have married him while he was in prison. Ricky didn't know that I was living with a man. I had told him that I loved him and would stay faithful to him and wait for him to get out of prison.

Despite what I was telling him, Ricky noticed the change in me and he didn't like it. Even though he smoked and had been high many times, he did not like the fact that I was smoking and getting high. I thought he was a hypocrite. He would call me his square baby, but I wanted to be hip. I thought it was an insult to be called square. I learned later that being "square" was what he admired and respected most about me. After eighteen months of a three-year sentence, Ricky was free and we resumed our relationship.

We couldn't go back to my mother's apartment, so for a short period of time we lived in a shooting gallery. This was a place where people came to shoot drugs. We found jobs earning minimum wages and Ricky continued to hustle. Ricky asked me if I would get pregnant again. I said that I would because we loved each other and we had vowed, even as children, that nothing would separate us except death. Today I think of how foolish and immature that decision was. We were not married and we had minimum wage jobs. Despite this, we had made our decision, and shortly after my 19th birthday, I was pregnant with our second child. Some time later, he told me that getting me pregnant was his strategy to keep me. He said he knew that if I had two of his children, I would never leave him. He found out that I had been with other men while he was in prison. I was honest with him and told him everything, and he forgave me.

I was into my second trimester when Ricky got caught on another theft charge. He was out on bail and awaiting trial when, in February of 1981, we decided that we wanted a new start. We wanted to leave the gang life behind and have a better life for our children. We decided to move to Milwaukee, Wisconsin.

Chapter Five

A New Start

My sister Pam had already told me that Jesus wanted to give me a better life and I needed to be saved. When she told me that Jesus loved me, I didn't want to hear it. I was angry with her because I felt she had abandoned the family. I felt more anger towards God for my horrible life. But now I was more vulnerable than ever. Ricky was facing more time in prison and I was expecting another baby. I cried out to God and started making my deals.

I had offered deals to God before. He had always come through on His end, but I had never kept my part of the deal. He had saved my life over and over again. One night I had been in a nightclub when someone started shooting through the window. I had crouched under a table, and glass was breaking all around me. The bullets were flying over my head, so I made a deal with God then and there, "Oh, please God, get me out of this without getting shot and I won't ever go to nightclubs again." God got me out alive, and I went right back to the nightclubs.

Another time, some drug dealers that I was living with had me try something new. The reaction to the drug they had given me left me so high that I was frightened. I tried to sleep it off, but this drug would not let me relax. There was nothing enjoyable about it. I stayed up all night and I remember praying, "God, if you get me off of this high, I swear I will never, ever get high again."

Eventually the high wore off and I was able to sleep. Although I refused to use that drug again, I used others and continued to get high.

Another time, some friends and I had been driving on the highway. We had all the windows rolled up and the car was filled with marijuana smoke. There were about five of us and we were all high. The driver lost control of the car. We were bouncing off the median and swerving all over the road, and I pleaded with God once again, "Please, help me live through this so I can turn my life over to you."

The driver regained control of the car, and I went on living my life no differently than I had before.

I had offered many deals to God, and He had always given me what I had asked for. He had certainly proven Himself to be faithful to me. I, on the other hand, had not followed through on anything I had ever promised Him. I called out to Him again as we went back for Ricky's trial in Chicago.

As I sat in the courtroom, waiting for the judge to read the verdict, I begged God, "Please God, don't let

Ricky go back to prison again. Please…I promise I will give you my life and never commit sexual sin again."

When the jury returned from deliberation, the judge read the verdict. "We find the defendant, Ricky Johnson…not guilty."

The jury had determined that Ricky was innocent, but we knew he was guilty. I knew then and there that God cared for me more than I had ever known or realized. I wasn't going to have to raise my children by myself. I could not possibly have been more grateful. We were heading back to Milwaukee to start our new life, and I would be true to the promise that I had made to God this time.

I didn't know anything about denominations or what type of church to go to, but I knew that I needed to get right with God. The very next Sunday after the trial, I began walking the streets of Milwaukee in search of a church.

BACK ON THE STREETS

Before I could even see the church, I could hear the music. There was singing and tambourines were playing. I decided to step inside and see a little more. The preacher was calling out, "Someone here has been playing with God, and this is your last chance to get right with Him. He won't tug on your heart anymore."

My own heart started pounding. The preacher went on to say, "You are fornicating, doing drugs and smoking, and now it's time to get right with God."

I was looking around, wondering who had told this man all of my business; after all, I was new to this city. He pleaded with the congregation to come and receive forgiveness and new life. I made my decision.

I wobbled my pregnant self up to the altar. I was the only one to respond to the call. I prayed as I had never prayed before. The pastor led me in a simple prayer that went something like this: "Dear Jesus, please forgive me for my sins. Thank you for dying on the cross and paying the price for my sins. I invite you into my heart and my life, in Jesus' name. Amen."

That day was the greatest day of my life! A promise made in a Chicago courtroom was fulfilled and my new life truly began.

I went home right after the service and found Ricky sitting at the kitchen table with some friends. They were playing cards, gambling and getting high. I walked in and yelled, "I'm saved! I'm SAVED!!"

Ricky looked up at me, smirked a little, and said, "That's good. Now don't mess up my high."

Later that night he found out just how serious I was. I kept my promise to God and refused to have sex with Ricky anymore. He couldn't understand. He said, "The damage is already done. You're already pregnant and we already have a child. What harm can I do now? Don't you love me?"

I told him that I loved him but that I loved Jesus more. Ricky didn't know about the deal I had made in the courtroom. After just a few days, Ricky proposed to me and we were married at the courthouse. I still remember the judge saying, "I sentence you two to live together for life, only to be separated by death."

I looked into Ricky's dark, beautiful eyes and saw the tears running down his cheeks. Those tears of joy started my own tears. After all those years, we were finally married. Later I would learn the Bible verse that states, "Be not unequally yoked with nonbelievers." (2 Corinthians 6:14)

I was trying to correct the sin of fornication (sex outside of marriage). That's why I married Ricky. I had vowed not to commit sexual sin anymore when I invited Jesus into my heart. Had I known God's standards for Christians marrying non-Christians, as much as I loved Ricky, I would not have married him.

A NEW START

I wanted to please my God, so I asked Him to deliver me from the drugs, alcohol, and nightclubs. He answered my prayer and immediately delivered me. I continued smoking for a few months because I had justified in my mind that there was no Bible verse that said thou shall not smoke. When I shared this with the young lady who was doing Bible study with me, she said no, there is no verse that says that thou shall not smoke, but there is a verse that says that your body is the temple of God (1 Corinthians 6:19) and that you are to present your body as a living sacrifice holy and acceptable to God (Romans 12:1). That night, when I picked up a cigarette to smoke, I was overwhelmed with the love of God. Thoughts of Jesus' love for me ran through my head. If Jesus loved me enough to give up His life for me, then I should love Him enough to be willing to give up smoking for Him. I prayed, "Lord, please deliver me from smoking." This addiction was more difficult than the drugs and alcohol. With each craving I would pray. The first day was the hardest. I had been told that if I would resist the devil, he would flee (James 4:7). I continued to resist the devil and smoking, and he did flee. Finally I was delivered from cigarettes.

Two months after my new life with Christ began, I gave birth to our daughter, Rickena. Ricky was thrilled to have a daughter, and I was thrilled to have a healthy baby. I had been worried about the drugs and the cigarettes that I had used during the pregnancy. I knew I had done a stupid, selfish thing by taking drugs while I was pregnant, but God was merciful and my baby was healthy and strong. To show my gratitude, I made a further resolve never to do drugs again.

I began to pray for employment. Neither of us had a high school diploma, so finding a job was a challenge. Eventually we both found jobs working at a knitting factory. I was happy to get off of welfare. I had vowed that my children would have a better life than I had. I worked the first shift and Ricky worked the second shift. We were grateful to be able to arrange our schedules to keep our children out of day care. Once we were settled, I sent for my brothers and sisters. I loved them too, and wanted so much more for them as well. I still had a mission to get my mom off of alcohol, so I moved her to Milwaukee along with my brothers and sisters. I believed that a new environment would help solve her drinking problem. Eventually I came to the realization that there was nothing I could do to stop her drinking. She needed an encounter with God.

Before long, she got her own place and her children left us and moved in with her. Her new environment made no difference, and she continued to drink. I was just grateful that she was close by and I could still look out for the children. They would often come by to eat, and to spend the night if things got bad at home. Mom received Social Security supplemental income payments for being an alcoholic, and I agreed to be her payee. She was still drinking heavily and would not have paid her bills without my help. I paid all of her bills with the money I received from her Social Security payments. I made sure that she was taken care of. I also made sure that my siblings' basic needs were met and that they would not become homeless.

I had learned from the Word of God that God had promised to meet all my needs. (Philippians 4:19) I now trusted God to do just that, and laid down the rules. There would be no more hustling or stealing to survive. God would take care of us. This was challenged when we were hungry and ran out of food. Ricky and my brothers were planning dinner when Ricky asked, "What do you guys have a taste for? I have a taste for some grilled steaks, greens and corn bread."

A NEW START

Ken was enthusiastic, "That sounds good to me!"

Tony agreed.

Ricky was coming up with a plan, "I will get the steaks. Ken and Tony, you guys hit the gardens and get the greens and see if you can get some green tomatoes too."

I couldn't keep quiet anymore, "Hold up, we are not going to be stealing anymore. We are going to trust God to provide for our needs."

Ricky jokingly said, "Well, while you're trusting God, I am going to help Him provide, so get the grill ready for some steaks."

When they got back with the stolen food, I refused to cook or eat any of it. They had to prepare the food themselves. That was the last time they stole food.

God did provide for us. We stayed around the corner from a church that served dinner nightly, so whenever we ran low on food we would stand in the soup line with all the other homeless and needy people. Although this was very humbling for me, I saw this as God's provision for me. I thanked God and was grateful.

As time went on, my faith grew. I loved Jesus more and more. I wanted everyone to experience this new life that I had, and I especially wanted it for Ricky. As I grew in my Christianity, Ricky fell harder into drugs. He held his job, but had started using a needle and his behavior was changing. I really wanted a Christian husband. I began praying intensely for Ricky, "God, please save and deliver Ricky."

One night, while Ricky and I were talking, I asked him if he wanted to receive Christ. He said, "Yes."

With great joy, I lead him in a prayer to receive Christ, but things were different for Ricky. He didn't experience the immediate deliverance that I had. I warned him that he shouldn't tell people he was a

Christian while he was living like a wicked sinner. Ephesians 4:1 says, "…to live a life worthy of the calling."

I knew that God's Word proclaimed that God disciplines those He loves. (Hebrews 12:6)

One evening, after I attended a Bible study, Ricky had come home high. I was hurt and disappointed, because he had promised me that he was really going to work at his relationship with God and attend church with me. Now he wanted money, and I wouldn't give it to him because I knew he would use it only to buy drugs. We had an argument and he said some really painful things to me. He called me a name that began with a "b" and my name begins with a "d". He spoke to me in a way he had never spoken to me before. Ricky had always treated me with great respect. I knew he respected my decision to follow Christ, so I couldn't understand his attitude. Our home had changed from a place where people used to get high and gamble, to a place where you couldn't do any of that anymore. Ricky had been the one to enforce this and he loved the fact that I was living for the Lord, so I was shocked that he had become so angry.

Immediately Ricky asked for forgiveness. I just sat there, hurt and shocked. He pleaded with me, over and over again, to forgive him, but I gave him the silent treatment. He continued to express how much he loved me and wanted to be forgiven, and I continued with the silent treatment. When he saw he could get nowhere with me, he left the house. I knew I should have forgiven him, but my pride had gotten in the way.

I just sat on the sofa after he left, thinking about what had just happened. Then I heard gunshots. I ran to the window and saw Ricky heading for the door. Before I could get to the door, Ricky was beating on it, calling out, "I've been shot! I've been shot!"

A NEW START

When I opened the door, I saw the gunman. After seeing me, he ran off down the alley. Ricky was leaning against the doorframe. He looked me in the eyes and calmly said, "Call the police, Baby. I am about to die."

Then my husband collapsed. I ran to the neighbor's house to call an ambulance, and when I got back to Ricky, he was lying in a pool of blood, convulsing. I knelt beside him and told him that he couldn't die, we needed him. Little Ricky was standing right there, and our sixteen-month-old daughter was in my arms. I pleaded with him to fight for Rickena. Ricky adored his daughter and each time I said her name, I could see him trying to get up. The paramedics finally came and worked on him before transporting us to the hospital.

We didn't have health insurance, so the paramedics took us to the county hospital, which was much farther away than the nearest hospital. The ride seemed to take forever, but when we finally arrived, they took Ricky into surgery right away. I sat in the waiting room and prayed. Thoughts of Ricky filled my mind. Would he have a long stay in the hospital? I was wondering whether there would be any permanent damage. I needed some support, so I made a couple of phone calls. First, I called the woman who had discipled me at my church. I was standing there shaking when I heard her answer the phone. With a quivering voice, I said, "Ricky's been shot. He's in surgery now."

There was a pause and she said, "What happened?"

I repeated that he had been shot and was now in surgery.

"Well, call me when he gets out of surgery and update me with his progress."

I just stood there with the phone in my hand, in disbelief of her response. I needed support, comfort, love. I certainly needed more than what she had offered.

I knew I had to keep going. I felt that if I were still for too long, I might explode, so I shook that off and tried again. This time I called a newer Christian, like myself. She barely let me get all the words out before she said, "What hospital are you in? I'll be right there."

Now there was nothing to do but sit, wait and pray. When the doctor finally came out, he simply said, "I'm sorry. We lost him in surgery. He really was fighting for his life, but the high alcohol levels in his blood caused him to bleed too much."

I couldn't believe what I was hearing. I asked if I could see my husband and the doctor said no, but I insisted on seeing my husband. I had started to make a big scene when the doctor reluctantly agreed to take me back to where Ricky was. I walked in and saw a gurney with a sheet spread over it. Someone was under it and, as I pulled back the sheet, I saw my husband's lifeless face. It was true. Ricky was dead.

I yelled at him, "This is not fair! Who is going to help me take care of our children? You just can't be dead! What am I going to do now?"

I began to weep uncontrollably, and the doctor ushered me back to the waiting room where my friend and her husband, along with Ricky's mother, were now standing. They had arrived while I was with Ricky and, when I saw his mother, I lost all my senses and became completely hysterical. She knew then, by my reaction, that her son was dead.

Eventually I calmed down just enough to tell her what had happened. We held each other for a while, and this mother who had just lost her son tried to comfort me. It was time to go home. It was time to tell my children that their daddy wasn't coming home.

A NEW START

Rickena was too young to understand. Little Ricky, on the other hand, knew what it meant when I told him that Daddy was dead and had gone to live with Jesus. Now it was my turn to hold and comfort my fatherless children. The days that followed are unclear in my memory. I do know that when I awoke the following morning and vaguely remembered the events of the day before, it all seemed like a bad dream, and then the dull ache began. I had to bury my best friend, and I knew that life would never be the same. We had lived together since I was fourteen. A part of me felt dead too. Ricky and I had talked about death before. We had both declared to each other that life would not be worth living if the other one had died. We had both said that if one of us died, the one left behind would kill themself to join the other. But because of my relationship with Jesus, I knew that life was worth living. But even with Jesus, it was a hard trial for me to bear. I cried myself to sleep many nights, wondering whether I would ever experience joy again in this life.

The church that I was a part of had the "somebodies" and the "nobodies." I was part of the "nobody" group. I was viewed as a "ghetto girl from the streets." There was no support in this group for a person like myself. I had been with the church for over a year, and not one fellow member came to Ricky's funeral. No meals or any other help that was normally given to widows in the church was given to me. God was my only comfort, and I could sense His love and concern for me.

I blamed myself for what had happened. I believed that if I had forgiven Ricky that night, as he had asked me to, maybe he wouldn't have left the house and he would still be alive. Of course, God did not expect me to carry that heavy guilt, and I eventually felt Him say,

"I am the giver of life. Many people have been shot and lived. I chose to bring Ricky home."

The Lord freed me from that overwhelming guilt.

I couldn't go back to work. I wanted to be home with my children. They had lost their daddy and I didn't want them to lose their mama too, so I chose to go back on welfare. This was so hard and humbling for me. I thought of going back to Chicago. I knew how to get a man to take care of me. In fact, one of the men I had known while Ricky was in prison had always told me I could come back to him anytime I wanted to. He had even said he would wait for me.

I started searching for his number. I looked all through the house and eventually found it in the back of a book. I knew he would be glad to hear from me because he had told me that he loved me. I started to anticipate hearing his voice and wondered what he would say to rescue me. I knew I was not in love with him, but

I would be safe and secure in his care. I picked up the phone, looked at the number, and began to dial. Before I could dial the last number, I stopped. I remembered my commitment to God. I had to stay true to Him and I wouldn't go back on my deal.

I hadn't yet learned many Bible scriptures, but one I had committed to memory was Romans 8:28: "And we know that in all things God works for the good of those who love Him, who have been called according to His purpose."

God used that verse to minister to me. I cried out to Him with tears streaming down my face, "God, I don't know how you are going to work this out for my good. You have taken my husband, my best friend, and the only person who has ever truly loved me. My children are now fatherless. With my natural eye, I just don't see this situation working for my good, but because your Word says it, I choose to believe."

A NEW START

As hard as it was, I did choose to believe.

Chapter Six

The Healing Begins

I grew as a Christian. I continued to go to the only church I had ever known. I was faithful in attending Bible study and Sunday services. I wanted to know my Lord and Savior better. Some people might wonder why I stayed at a church that saw me and treated me as a "ghetto girl from the streets." My answer is simple: It wasn't God who had done me wrong, it was the people.

I still needed that church because it was the only place where I knew I could learn more about the Word of God.

There was no one for me to depend on or trust except for God and his Word. He began showing me, even in "small" ways, that I could count on Him to be faithful. Ricky had died in November of 1982. My children and I did not have warm winter coats and boots that year, and I couldn't afford to buy them. I remember (and records show) that December was the warmest winter month that Milwaukee, Wisconsin, had seen in decades. I just knew that God was on my side. When the Lord did bless me with some unexpected money for winter clothes, only then did the weather turn cold. I was amazed. God loved me enough to hold back cold weather until my children and I were prepared. I thought, "What an awesome, personal and powerful God I serve!"

I was learning God's Word and *seeing it come alive in my life*. I knew then that I would never leave my God. He gave me a promise that He would never leave or forsake me. I could never leave or forsake Him either. God and I were now a team. I had no one else. My relationship with God is what had kept me sane when Ricky died. It's also how I knew when things were not quite right.

I got to a certain point in my walk with the Lord where I knew that something was wrong. I couldn't sense God's presence the way I had in the past. I had learned in Bible study that sin hinders our relationship with God (Isaiah 59:2). I wondered whether I had any unconfessed sin in my life. I asked God for some answers, and He began speaking to my heart. I heard Him say, "Unforgiveness."

I thought I was ready to hear the rest. "Okay, God, who do I need to forgive?"

His answer was very clear, "You need to forgive your mother."

I was shocked and complained to Him, "You're the sovereign God. You saw everything my mother did and said to me. You should understand why I hate her. She abandoned me! Because of her negligence, I was sexually abused. I couldn't finish high school because I had to take care of her children. She didn't love me. Why should I forgive her?"

He was firm in his reply, "You have to forgive your mother if you want to continue in a relationship with me. Unforgiveness is a sin. It is now time to forgive your mother."

I had just admitted to hating my mother. I didn't want to forgive her, but I did want to stay close to my Lord, so I replied, "Well, it is your will that I forgive my mother and, even though I don't want to do this, I do want your will for my life."

Then I made a conscious decision to forgive my mother, and asked God to help me with the process. He revealed to me that if I were willing, He would give me the strength to forgive. Forgiving and loving my mom was a process. It did not happen overnight, but eventually my emotions caught up with my decision to forgive.

In 1997 Mom was diagnosed with cancer and given three months to live. She had moved back to Memphis. Two of my brothers and two sisters were already living there. When I received word that Mom was dying, I took money from my small savings and picked her up and took her on a vacation to Florida. She lived two years longer than the doctors had expected her to live. That was the longest time I had known her to be sober. She had asked for forgiveness from my two older sisters, so while we were on vacation, I was waiting for her to ask me for forgiveness also. But she never asked me to forgive her, and I never knew why. Mom died January 20, 1999. I was so glad that I had already chosen to forgive her. I had no regrets. I felt free.

After some time passed, the Lord revealed to me that my dad was another person whom I needed to forgive and release. Mom had an excuse because she was an alcoholic. That prevented her from being a good mom, but I could not understand my dad. He had no excuse for turning his back on me. I had suffered hunger, lived in horrible conditions, and worn raggedy clothes. All the while, he wore $500 suits, drove a new Cadillac each year, and lived in a nice house in the suburbs. He hadn't been there to protect me from all the men who had taken advantage of me all those years.

Again, the forgiveness was a process. I also had to accept that not only was my dad negligent in my childhood, but neither was he a dad to me in my adult years, nor a grandfather to my children. Although I still loved and forgave my dad, I had to let go of all the expectations that he was still not fulfilling. My heavenly Father's love would have to be enough. After forgiving my dad, God gave me the privilege of leading my dad in prayer to receive Christ.

Finally, I knew the time had come that I would have to forgive the man who had murdered my husband. The Bible tells us to pray for our enemies. One day, I was praying for the young man and I told God that if the opportunity presented itself, I would share Jesus with him. Of course, the opportunity did present itself. One day I was in the barbershop with my son. Little Ricky was getting a haircut when the man who had shot Big Ricky walked in. He came and sat down beside me. My heart started racing. I prayed to God, "Lord, please help me," and I began talking to the young man. "I know you don't remember me, but I'm Ricky Johnson's wife."

A flicker of recognition flashed across his face and I could see fear. I quickly added, I'm not trying to re-open the case."

He looked nervous, but stayed where he was and listened to what else I had to say, "I wonder how you sleep at night, knowing you have murdered someone's husband, father, brother and son. I would just like to know, for my own information, why did you shoot him?"

All he said was, "I didn't do it."

I patiently told him, "Remember, I was there."

Surprisingly, he still didn't move, so I continued, "I forgive you and, more importantly, Jesus loves you and offers forgiveness if you'll just ask for it."

We talked for a while and, as we did, I could see him relax and open up more. I did not have the privilege of leading the young man to Christ that day, but I left the barbershop a free woman. I had done as God wanted me to do. None of the people I had to forgive said that they were sorry or apologized to me in any way, but it didn't matter. I knew that I needed to forgive, and when I didn't have the strength to do it on my own, God was there to make me strong. Forgiveness allowed me to begin my journey to healing.

Although it may be hard to believe sometimes, God does not ever give us more than we can handle together with Him. God did not overwhelm me with the healing process. He revealed my pain to me a little at a time when He knew I was ready to deal with it. I then received healing, one layer at a time, until I had received deep, complete healing. Even as I write this book, I am still receiving deeper healing in some areas of my life.

The journey continued as I was attending and speaking at a "Healing for Your Heart Conference" sponsored by Discipleship Unlimited in Milwaukee. I heard the banquet speaker say that there were some of us who were angry with God because we didn't have His perspective on our situation. We felt that He wasn't there for us. The speaker challenged us to ask God to give us His perspective of our hurts and disappointments from our past. I had to admit that I was angry with God. I started to pray, "Why couldn't I have had a normal family? Where were you when I was hungry and went for days without food? What about the times I had been abused? Why did I have to live in condemned buildings?"

God had an answer, "You're alive now because I preserved you."

In my mind I saw a clear picture of the fire hydrant that ran a constant stream of water when we had no water in our apartment. God continued to speak to me, "Your childhood was training for the ministry that I have called you to."

I knew then that God had not caused my pain. The anger left immediately. We cannot escape the sinful world we live in, or the sinners in it. He had allowed me to go through all I went through and could use now to glorify Him. My misery had been training for my ministry. I now understood my sensitivity to the homeless, drug addicts, teen moms, widows, the poor, and abused children. I could relate to them because of my own life. I had been in all those places in my life. It was all beginning to make sense, and my vision was becoming clearer. Now it was time to move forward with His plan for my life.

Chapter Seven

Remarried

The effects of the sexual abuse that I suffered haunted me for countless years. I did not trust people. Normal hugs and kisses from people still felt wrong and even dirty to me. I did not enjoy any kind of physical intimacy, even with Ricky, the man I loved and adored. It became more of an obligation or something I had to endure. It affected my relationships. I asked God for healing.

I'm not sure when it happened exactly, but one day someone gave me a hug and it didn't feel wrong. I was able to embrace people without feeling overly cautious or violated. I knew that this was what God intended for intimacy and that I deserved to experience the love that people had for me in a pure and Godly way. I also needed to be able to return that love. I knew that I needed healing because I did not want to go into another marriage until I could love and accept love the way that God intended.

Being single was a real challenge for me. I had not been without a guy since I was 14 years old, and now I had two little ones to care for by myself. I carried a tremendous amount of shame from the past. I thought that I was ugly. I had very low self-esteem and didn't like much about myself. To tell the truth, I hated myself. I often thought that no one would ever want to marry me with my history and two small children. I prepared myself for the possibility that I might never marry again. At around this time, a young Christian man proposed to me. I accepted, thinking this might be my only chance. He was a wonderful man, sweet, kind and Godly. Eventually we both knew this was not God's will for our lives and broke the engagement. I would have rather remained single for the rest of my life than to marry outside of God's will. I began to get busy doing God's work. I loved to share the gospel, and was always sharing Jesus with people. That's when I met Maurice Ross.

We were in the same Bible study and we were involved in a singles' fellowship. It was not love at first sight. I was sure he wouldn't be interested in someone like me, and I knew he didn't like children. I thought he was a nice guy but a bit snobbish. Our backgrounds were very different. He grew up in a stable, two-parent home. He was raised in the church, where his dad was a deacon and his mother was a Sunday School teacher. He and his brothers sang in the choir and had formed their own singing group. There was no way that a guy like Maurice would ever even consider a woman like me.

BACK ON THE STREETS

One day, a group of us singles were down at the lake. I was sharing Jesus with a young lady, talking to her about surrendering her life to Him. I tried quoting certain scriptures to answer her questions. Whenever I got stuck and didn't know where to find certain verses, Maurice would step in with the right scripture and answer her question. I started to look at him in a new light. Maybe God meant for us to be together as ministry partners and even as marriage partners. I began to pray about this and to my surprise, God said, "Yes."

I was so excited that I shared my good news with a friend, but I didn't dare share it with Maurice. I believed that if it was His will, God would reveal it to Maurice. We began dating. Christian dating was very different than the dating I had experienced in my past. We fell in love, but we didn't fall into bed.

At the time, Maurice worked the third shift, so it was not unusual for him to call me early in the morning.

REMARRIED

One morning at about five, Maurice called and said, "I love you, let's go to the courthouse and get married."

God had revealed His will to Maurice! I was so excited and joyously said, "Yes!" The excitement kept me from going back to sleep. Maurice got to my apartment that morning shortly after eight. We went downtown to get a marriage license, but I needed a death certificate and a copy of my birth certificate before they would give us the license. I had the death certificate, but I didn't have my birth certificate. Maurice suggested that we should drive to Chicago, get my birth certificate, and come back to Milwaukee to get married. So we went to Chicago, and on the drive back I kept thinking of how I couldn't believe that I was going to marry Maurice! My thoughts were, "Rapture, please do not come today." We arrived back at the courthouse just five minutes before their offices closed. The clerk remembered us, "Boy, you guys must really want to get married!"

It was so close to closing time that we could not get married at the courthouse, so we took our license back to my apartment. There we called a minister friend and asked him to come over and marry us. He agreed, and we were married that same day. Having kept my commitment to God to stay sexually pure made me feel like a virgin bride.

Maurice was a real gentleman and rather cute too. I was so pleased with God's selection for me and for the children. Ricky had been praying for a daddy and Rickena was still too young to understand what was going on. Maurice grew to love my children as his own, and they knew and loved him as their father. Maurice and I had three more children together, and the man who at one time didn't want any children now had five of his own. Our relationship together continued to grow, and so did our relationship with God. For our fifth anniversary, we renewed our vows.

Maurice led family Bible studies. We prayed together and grew closer as a family. I began to teach the children as well. I wanted my children to know and love the Lord as much as I did, if not more.

When you are left to raise yourself and have no role models, it leaves you unprepared for life. There were simple things that I needed to know and learn, such as taking care of a house, manners, and etiquette. I needed help to be a Godly wife and mother. I was years into my walk with Jesus when, standing over a toilet, dipping a dirty cloth diaper, I complained in frustration, "Lord, I know that your Word tells the older women to teach the younger women. I have been praying for quite some time now, asking you to give me an older woman to teach me how to be a good wife and mother. I'm still waiting!"

He replied, "I have answered your prayer. 'Though my father and mother forsake me, the Lord will take me up.' (Psalms 27:10) I decided to teach you Myself so that no one would be able to take credit for your life but Me."

When I thought about it, I could see how God had taught me many things, as well as developed my parenting skills. He had taught me how to be a wife. I am still learning how to keep the house organized. Actually, I am waiting for God to bless me with a maid. In desperation, I had been crying out daily to Him for wisdom in taking care of the children, my husband, and running the house. Daily, He was answering my prayer. I was doing it. I had no one to thank but God.

I had certain behaviors that I did not understand. I had no problem investing money in my home or my family. Whenever I had the money to do so, I would buy things to fix up the house, and I saw to it that my husband and children always had nice wardrobes and would always look nice. But for myself I bought the bare necessities. I kept myself clean, but had a very small, simple and inexpensive wardrobe with one pair of black, all-purpose shoes.

One day I was out shopping for my girls' winter coats. They always wore nice wool dress coats that were rather costly, but I didn't mind paying the extra money. I wanted my girls to look nice because their physical appearance was important to me. I walked through the store and saw a coat for myself and tried it on. I liked the coat, but thought it was too expensive although it was the same price that I was willing to pay for my girls' coats.

God began to speak to me, "Why are you willing to pay that amount of money for your girls and not for yourself?"

The answer was that I did not feel worthy. In fact, I did not like myself. I felt ugly and cheap. Whenever I was around pretty or educated women, these thoughts would rise up and feelings of inferiority would overwhelm me. God began to encourage me. He said that I was fearfully and wonderfully made. (Psalms 139:14) He also reminded me that He was the King of Kings and because I was his daughter, I was royalty! (1 Peter 2:9) I received it and began to walk as a daughter of royalty. The Lord took away the low self-esteem and replaced it with Christ-esteem. My husband and children had to get used to the new me. Now when I shop for myself, they say that I was "overhealed."

As my passion to raise a Godly family grew, the Lord presented a new challenge to me. He was calling me to homeschool my children. The thought of doing such a thing so overwhelmed me that I ignored it for a year or so. It was my concern for their spiritual growth that softened my heart. The Lord continued to lay homeschooling on my heart. I told God, "I can't homeschool. I never graduated from high school. I'm not smart enough."

God told me, "You serve a God who knows everything. 'If any man lacks wisdom, let him ask of God.'" (James 1:5)

I knew there was no way to escape doing what God was calling me to do. I had to be obedient to God, so I went to Maurice, who at first did not agree with the idea. I continued to pray. Eventually, after much prayer, Maurice did agree that we should homeschool. I began that adventure with total dependence on God, and we were shocked at the results.

Our children were excelling both spiritually and academically. Whenever I came across some schoolwork that I didn't understand, I would pray for God to help me understand it, and He did. He showed Himself to be faithful to our family. The children knew God as 'One who even helps with schoolwork.' I wanted the children to be well–rounded, so we added music to their studies. We had to take them out for their music lessons, and they developed a love for music. They began requesting different instruments. We prayed and made financial sacrifices to make sure that they had the instruments they needed. When they needed money for lessons, God provided that too, and when there wasn't money for lessons, God provided instructors who were willing to give their time and talent.

Although I had forgiven my mom and dad over the years, I would have different situations or events that would trigger my painful past, and I would have to choose to continue to forgive. For example, my parents were not there for the birth of any of my children, not even a visit to the hospital, and when my children had special occasions to celebrate, there were no grandparents around to celebrate with us. My daughter Chaunte won a competition and was to be one of the featured soloists to play with the Milwaukee Symphony Orchestra. Many of the other parents who had entered their children in the competition could play the piano well enough to accompany their children. I felt that Chaunte was at a disadvantage because I had no training in music. I couldn't play any instrument, and I began to feel angry with my mom and dad all over again.

I had renewed memories of wanting to play the piano as a child. As a girl, I would play the edge of the table as though it were a piano and the broom as though it were my guitar. Dad wasn't there, and Mom was never sober long enough to invest in my dreams and passions. Dad could have afforded lessons and Mom had enough music training that she could have been my music teacher. In fact, Mom had such a good upbringing that it left me with not only anger, but many questions as well.

I brought those questions before God. What would my life have been like had my mom not been an alcoholic? What if Dad had stayed? Would I have been a great musician? Would I have been a teen mom? What college would I have attended? Would I have been financially stable? Where and who would I be today? Had my parents robbed me of my heritage?

God reminded me of a promise that He had given me years ago. "I will restore to you the years that the locusts have eaten." (Joel 2:25)

"When?" was the question I had for Him.

"Deborah, look around, you are in a season of receiving restoration now. Look at your life."

He was right. I could see it. All of my children played multiple instruments, just like my mom. In fact, God had gifted all of the children. Although I could not accompany Chaunte or teach her, she played as well as the other children. She had won! I began to see restoration in many other areas as well, and still look forward to even more restoration.

The girls formed a string quartet with two violins, a viola, and a cello. They are known as Sisters of PraiZe. They began receiving invitations to churches, conferences, retreats, weddings, and all types of functions. God's plan was revealing itself more and more. Although I never finished high school, I have graduated three of my homeschooled children and sent them to college. I have homeschooled our children for fifteen years. Whenever I complain about not finishing high school, my oldest daughter says to me, "Mom, you have sent three children to college. Give yourself a diploma."

Chapter Eight

On the Streets Again

"The Spirit of the Sovereign Lord is upon me, because the Lord has anointed me to preach good news to the poor. He has sent me to bind up the brokenhearted, to proclaim freedom for the captives and release from darkness for the prisoners." (Isaiah 61:1)

My passion for evangelism, along with love and concern for people, began to grow. I wanted people to experience the same type of relationship that I had with God. I wanted them to understand that He could heal the deepest of pain. He offers a better life for those who trust in Him. He offers a life of peace, forgiveness, acceptance and purpose. With this growing passion, I began to pray, "Lord please help me to get this good news to people." Whenever or wherever I met people, I told them how much Jesus loved them and that He wanted to have a relationship with them. After much prayer, the Lord laid it on my heart to take our battery-operated karaoke machine out to the park and let the children sing and play their instruments. As the children sang, people began to crowd around and listen. When the crowd had finished growing, I stood on a picnic table and began to tell them how Jesus had made a difference in my life. I then invited them to surrender their lives to Christ and begin a relationship with Him. I was amazed at the response. Men, women, boys, girls and even gang bangers came and surrendered their lives to Jesus. God began to give me a clear vision for a street ministry.

Maurice and I were so excited. We knew that God's Word tells us, "Go to the highways and byways and compel them to come in that His house may be filled." (Luke 14:23)

Compelling them to come was deep in my spirit. I prayed, "Lord, how do you want us to compel them to come?"

He reminded me of my days of being hungry and needy, and then He said, "Love them by meeting some basic needs first. Then tell them that I love them and desire a relationship with them."

I could envision us feeding the hungry before sharing the gospel. God was calling us to do this on a larger and more organized scale. We would need a great deal of money to carry out this vision. I continued to pray, and even wrote down the vision and all that we would need to make it happen. God was calling us to be missionaries to the cities across America. I drew a picture of a motor home pulling a portable stage, and made a list of everything we would need to carry out the vision. The list consisted of a sound system, chairs, tents, popcorn popper, portable stove, Bibles, keyboard, tracts, and enough financial support to become full-time missionaries to the cities across America.

We did not wait until all the items came in to get started. We just continued to go with our instruments and karaoke machine. One day we were in the parks when it began to rain, and we almost lost the little equipment that we had. We rushed everything into our van and praised God that our equipment had not been damaged. When a friend heard what had happened, she wrote out a check and told us to buy a canopy to protect the equipment and instruments.

We continued to pray for all the items on the prayer list. God was faithful to us. Each item we received has its own testimony of how God blessed us. I like the story of how we got the sound system, motor home, and the portable stage which is now our "church on wheels."

BACK ON THE STREETS

One day we received a phone call and someone asked, "What one thing do you really need for your ministry?" I asked Maurice, and he said we really needed a sound system. We were told to price what we needed, which we did, and they sent us a check to cover the cost and we now had our new sound system!

A benefit concert was held to raise money for the "church on wheels." It was a great concert. The children sang and played their instruments along with other talented singers and musicians. At the end of the evening, there still was not enough money to buy the eight-thousand-dollar unit. I felt very discouraged. People would give far more to foreign missionaries, but we were just city missionaries. Did the church even care about the people in the city? I was having lunch with a friend one day when out of the blue, she asked how much money we needed to get the unit. I told her our amount, and the check was written for the amount needed. Praise God! We finally were able to purchase the "church on wheels." God had answered yet another prayer!

We pulled the "church on wheels" with our full-size conversion van. After a while, the weight of the stage began to damage the engine. Our family van died. To continue the ministry, we would need a much larger engine to pull the stage. We began to pray intensely for a motor home. We even went out to price brand-new motor homes. That's when we realized that this was a God-size task. My faith was strong because of what I had already seen God do. By now we were receiving calls to do outreaches out of state. During the first two years, we had to rent motor homes for out-of-state travel.

Through our newsletter, we put the word out that we needed a motor home to continue the ministry. Money came in, but not enough to purchase the motor home. Some people told us that maybe God didn't want us to be missionaries, while others told us where we could find a used motor home. We knew we needed a new motor home with a custom design to fit our large family, and a warranty that comes with a new model because of the distances we would travel. This custom unit would cost us a great deal of money. We continued to pray.

Finally we had enough money to make a down payment to finance the motor home. We went to the bank to complete the paperwork and secure the loan. We were amazed when the president of the bank *donated* ten thousand dollars so that our payments would be more manageable. He told us that he believed in what we were doing. Now we were free to do God's work.

In the beginning, when we did outreach in the parks, there was no plan for follow-up and discipleship.

This bothered Maurice and me. Who would help the people grow in their new faith? We prayed, and the vision became clearer. God was calling us to partner with churches. Many churches stay small because they will not go out to the highways and byways and compel people to come. We put together some basic evangelism training and orientation for the outreach. We even had a plan for follow-up. Churches welcomed us with open arms. They now had the help they needed to reach the communities that surrounded their churches; we had the help we needed for doing our outreach and making sure churches would care for their new Christians.

Now we set up the "church on wheels" on the grounds of churches. We set up carnival-style with popcorn poppers, tents, and a portable stove to cook hot dogs. We serve a simple meal to the people while they listen to music and life-changing testimonies. The gospel is always presented, giving people an opportunity to receive Christ.

Our holiday promotional outreaches come from some of my own painful experiences. In August we do back-to-school outreaches. Each child is given a new backpack filled with school supplies. I never had a backpack. I carried my books in a plastic grocery bag that had been doubled for strength. It brings me great joy to help bless the children, because I know many of them are coming from homes like the one I was raised in.

The areas that we go into are poverty stricken. One or both of the parents are on drugs or alcohol, and the children suffer. For Easter and Thanksgiving, we give away turkeys and ham with trimmings. From my own experience, I know that there were many times we would not have eaten had people not given us food. During the Christmas outreach, we give away toys. We added knitwear because at the first Christmas outreach, the children were not properly dressed for the weather. Now we dress the children in warm hats, scarves and gloves while serving hot drinks and cookies. God's Word tells us that the harvest is plentiful but the laborers are few. We have seen the plentiful harvest and have witnessed the multitudes come to Christ.

Chapter Nine

He Has a Plan for You Too

The pain and disappointments of life can leave us feeling hopeless and as though we have no future. The Bible says, "'For I know the plans I have for you,' declares the Lord, 'plans to prosper you and not to harm you, plans to give you hope and a future.'" (Jeremiah 29:11)

"The devil's plan is to kill, steal and destroy lives." (John 10:10) When we don't live a life that is surrendered to Christ, the doors are open for the evil one to come in and destroy our lives. Maybe life has been good to you but you still have a void. That void can be filled only by Jesus Christ.

God's plan for you is as simple as ABC.

<u>A</u>dmit that you're a sinner.

All have sinned. Romans 5:12 tells us that sin entered the world through one man and that man was Adam.

One may say, "I am not a bad person and therefore I deserve to go to heaven." We are all from the seed of Adam; therefore, we were born with this condition called sin. Romans 6:23 says that the earning of sin is death. The type of death that the Bible talks about is to be eternally separated from God in hell.

Revelation 20:15 states, "If anyone's name was not found written in the book of life, he was thrown into the lake of fire."

In 2 Thessalonians 1:8, 9, it says, "He will punish those who do not know God and do not obey the gospel of our Lord Jesus. They will be punished with everlasting destruction and shut out from the presence of the Lord and from the majesty of his power."

Many of us have the wrong picture of hell. I did. I thought that I would be there to party with my friends or that I would just burn up and be finished with existence. But that is not what will happen, because we are eternal beings, which means we will live forever. The question is where will we spend eternity, in heaven or in hell?

The choice is ours. We have to turn from our sins and turn to Jesus. This process is called repenting.

Believe Jesus paid the price for your sins.

The Bible tells us that the devil and his demons believe (James 2:19), so it's not enough to say, "I believe." You have to receive what Christ did for you. This requires faith. "But God demonstrates his own love for us in this: While we were still sinners, Christ died for us." (Romans 5:8) Jesus paid the price for our sins.

We all deserve hell, but Jesus loves us so much that He created a way for us to escape hell. The Bible tells us, "God so loved the world that He gave his one and only son, that whoever believes in Him shall not perish [and go to hell] but have eternal life." (John 3:16)

Choose to repent and confess Him as Lord of your life.

"That if you confess with your mouth, 'Jesus is Lord,' and believe in your heart that God raised him from the dead, you will be saved." (Romans 10:9)

Choose to believe and receive what Jesus did on the cross as payment for your sins. Again, the choice is ours. Jesus will not force his way into our lives. We have to open the doors of our hearts and let Him in. Don't confuse religion with relationship. The fact that you go to church or were raised in the church does not mean that you are in a relationship with God, just as being raised in a garage does not make you a car. If you cannot remember a time in your life when you chose to turn away from your sins and turn to Jesus by receiving Him as Lord and Savior, I encourage you to not put it off any longer.

Choose to invite Him into your heart and into your life. Begin a relationship with Him by making Him your Lord (boss) and Savior (the one who can save your soul from hell). If you want to begin a relationship with Jesus, you can pray your own prayer right now, in your own words, or you can pray this prayer:

"Dear Jesus, thank you for dying on the cross just for me. Please forgive me for my sins and forgive me for trying to live a life apart from you. I turn from my sins and I turn to you. Please come into my heart and life. Be my Lord (meaning take charge of my life) and my Savior (save me from hell), in Jesus' name. Amen."

HE HAS A PLAN FOR YOU TOO

This prayer is not magical, so if you prayed it and were not sincere and did not exercise faith, nothing has happened. But if you were sincere and exercised faith, congratulations! You are now part of God's family! Oh, what a blessing to have your sins forgiven and to receive the free gift of eternal life! When you invited Jesus into your heart and into your life, his Holy Spirit came to live inside of you. The Holy Spirit is there to lead you and to help you to overcome any sin. The Holy Spirit is there also to teach, comfort and heal you.

Now that you are a babe in Christ, you need to grow and mature. If you were to bring home a newborn baby from the hospital and never feed the baby, the baby would die. In the same way, if you are not fed spiritually, you will die spiritually. There are three things you need to do in order to grow and mature in your Christian walk.

1. The first thing is **prayer.** The Bible tells us to always pray. (1 Thessalonians 5:17) Prayer is the way we communicate with God. Prayer is not only talking to God, but it is also listening to God. He wants to commune with us. Prayer strengthens our relationship with God and helps us to discern the voice of Satan from our own and God's voice.

2. The second thing we must do is **fellowship** with other Christians. (Hebrews 10:25) Fellowshipping with older Christians will strengthen you. Since association brings assimilation, you want to find Christians who are Christlike.

3. The third thing we need to do is **study God's Word**. (2 Timothy 2:15) Pray, and ask God to lead you to a church where the Word of God is not only taught, but is also lived. The Bible is our manual for life.

God has a plan for your life, just as He had a plan for mine. "He brought me up out of a horrible pit, out of the miry clay, and set my feet upon a rock and established my goings." (Psalms 40:2)

Chapter Ten

Stories for His Glory

From Hopeless to Hopeful

My name is Trina, and I am from a dysfunctional family. I have suffered all kinds of abuse, verbal, physical, and sexual. The unbearable pain caused me to be a very angry, violent, and untrusting person. To deal with this pain, I would fight anybody about anything. As a young teenager, I began looking for love in all the wrong places. I began drinking, popping pills, smoking cigarettes, and eventually doing crack cocaine. When I was fourteen years old, I became a teen mom. By the time I was seventeen, I had three children. I didn't stop until I had given birth to six children.

From my fighting and cocaine use, I would be in and out of jail while my children were in and out of different foster care homes. I was destroying all of our lives. While pregnant with the sixth child, I was arrested on a charge for which there was no bail. I had to do some time.

The child was taken from me immediately after the birth. During my incarceration, I asked God to forgive me and received Jesus as my Lord and personal Savior. I began studying his Word and I began to grow, but I still had a lot of anger. I saw the hypocrites in the body of Christ and began to get tired of Christians.

During my incarceration, Pastor Deborah came to the prison with Discipleship Unlimited. She did a song in sign language and preached a powerful message on forgiveness that challenged me to address my fellow inmates. God led me to ask my sisters "behind the wall" for forgiveness.

Before Pastor Deborah left the prison, she approached me with insight as to what God was doing in my life. She gave me the name of the church that she was attending and told me to contact her there when I was released. I was in awe because this lady had delivered the Word of God with authority. No one had opened up to me the way she had. I could relate to her. I felt that she was real, and she left me with the assurance that I was more than a number. She was an example of Jesus in the flesh for me.

Upon my release, I had some doubts about contacting Pastor Deborah. I was tired of fake Christians. However, I had a major trial that I was facing. Getting my children back was a huge challenge for me. I knew that God was with me, but I needed a human being to coach me. I needed to learn more about the Christian process and how to become a Godly mom. I still had a lot of anger, and was in need of healing and deliverance. The mentor/mentee relationship began.

Because of my past issues, there were times that I tried to step out of the relationship and back into my old life. I would get discouraged dealing with the court system and trying to get my children back. I had to start from scratch, get a job, find an apartment, and then furnish it. Pastor Deborah pursued me with love. She was determined that I was not going back into the street life. She told me that my children were also hurting and needed their mom, a holy, healed and delivered mom. She reminded me that God was in control of my children, and not the courts. She said that if we prayed and I did my part, then God would do his part.

God answered our prayers. I found a job and Pastor Deborah held my money until I had saved enough to get an apartment and furnish it. My children were placed back with me. Pastor Deborah always reminds me that God has a plan for me and my children. I am learning to humble myself and be accountable--and to trust. Pastor Deborah lived the life of abuse, drugs and alcohol. She overcame, was delivered from those circumstances, and now walks with the Lord. I have concluded that Pastor Deborah is living where I have been trying to go.

Trina Anderson
Milwaukee, Wisconsin

From the 'Burbs to the Streets

Who would have guessed that two little girls growing up with totally different backgrounds would one day become women who would cross paths in such a profound way? Only an all-knowing God could plan such an event.

"'For I know the plans I have for you,' says the Lord. 'They are plans for good and not for disaster, to give you a future and a hope.'" (Jeremiah 29:11)

One of the girls was raised in poverty with an alcoholic mom and a negligent dad, and often wondered where her next meal would come from. The other girl was raised in middle-class suburbia with a loving mom and supportive dad, and never wondered whether or not there would be food on the table.

Deborah and I come from very different backgrounds, but God brought us together to carry out His will and accomplish His purposes. I don't remember when we first met. We knew of each other from different church events and would see each other from time to time.

In February of 1996, Deborah and Maurice were conducting their parenting classes, "Raising a Godly Seed," at New Testament Church. It was during those classes that I began to understand and know Deborah's heart. Her passion for strengthening and equipping parents to raise Godly children was so evident. I was encouraged to find someone who shared some of the same values as mine concerning family and children. The parenting classes were right on target for me, and provided the confirmation I needed in some areas and education in others.

A few months after the parenting classes, Deborah invited me to take part in a Bible study that she was holding in her home. The Bible study lasted twelve weeks, and it was during that time that a friendship began to develop. In time, Deborah began to share her passion for lost souls and vision for street evangelism.

As I reflect back, I think it was probably my friendship with Deborah that helped me understand the concept of street evangelism. My God-given temperament is somewhat introverted, so the idea of taking the gospel of Jesus Christ to the streets was intimidating!! I had no idea of what to expect. Would I be rejected? Would I be safe? What would I say? What could I do? Fear would try to keep me from venturing out of my comfort zone, but God's Word assured me that I could do all things through Him. (Philippians 4:13)

The first time I went to the streets, I was amazed that people would actually come and participate in an "outdoor" church service, especially since it was in the winter! But they did come, and stood in the cold to hear the life-changing news about how much Jesus loved them and how He had died for them! When Deborah gave the invitation to accept Christ, I was overwhelmed at the response! Young and old, men and women, boys and girls responded to the invitation to accept the free gift of salvation!! I began to look into the faces and eyes of the crowd, and I saw people with hurting hearts searching for hope. As I prayed with some of them, I began to realize that while we may have different life experiences, we all have the same need for Jesus.

As I reflect on the years of my friendship with Deborah, I am amazed and awed by the work of God in her life. The very incidents of her life that could have destroyed her are the very things God uses to draw people closer to Him so they can experience his transforming grace in their lives. Only an all-knowing God would use a girl from the streets to draw a girl from the suburbs back to the streets to give hope to a hurting world.

Desiree Hoard
Brookfield, Wisconsin

The Adoption

Mark and I were ready to adopt back in 1988. We had decided that we would like to take so-called "hard-to-place" American children, since we had three children of our own. Of course, that led us to African-American children.

As we were going through the process of adoption, we moved to a white rural area in Southeastern Wisconsin at the same time a biracial baby boy needed a home. Milwaukee County officials wanted to know how we could ever give this child a sense of his racial identity, and our agency suggested we develop some relationships with African-American families.

That was something we were only too happy to pursue, so we called a black pastor we were familiar with and explained the need. He gave us the names of several families in his congregation. I called the first pair of names on the list: Deborah and Maurice Ross. I never got to any of the other names because after that first hour-long conversation, I began to attend Bible studies in the Rosses' home. We developed a beautiful friendship with the whole family. They rejoiced with us when God answered our prayer and our baby boy was placed in our home.

Sometime after our second African-American baby boy had been placed in our home, Deborah invited me to a women's retreat where she had an opportunity to speak. On the way home, she shared that she believed God was calling her to a public speaking ministry. I looked at my friend, whom I knew at one time some people would have classified as a "nobody." Now she was "somebody" in Christ, and I had seen the impact of her faith on the people around her. Even though at that time *I* didn't see the makings of a public speaker, I did see a relationship with God that was sweet, simple, and very deep. I knew that if Deborah said God was calling her, all I had to do was sit back and watch a ministry unfold.

Soon after that, Deborah called me and excitedly told of sharing the Gospel in the park and seeing the people who were hungry for God respond. We rejoiced with them. At the same time, the Ross children were beginning their music lessons and we saw a way we could help prepare them for ministry, so we underwrote some of the music training.

As Deborah's vision for a ministry grew, the need for a trailer that could also serve as a stage became clear. God had blessed us financially at about that time, and we were able to contribute towards the trailer, as well as serve on the board. JohnRoss Ministries was launched.

Through our friendship with the Ross family, we have been blessed. Being involved with them and the African-American community has also been a blessing for our entire family that now includes five African-American children. We remain committed to the belief that black and white people can, and should, work together to build the Kingdom of God.

Judie Raether
Rubicon, Wisconsin

From Broken to Whole

My name is Leila Newman. I am a single mom, raised in holiness with generations of bishops, pastors and ministers in my family. My father was a pastor and a bishop, so my home was a strict, no-nonsense kind of atmosphere. Yet, I was not shielded from life's blows and disappointments. I went through pain and hurt that I thought was reserved only for sinners. God's blessings come to us in so many ways, and they're often unexpected but very timely.

Deborah Ross came into my life in 1997, at a time when I was experiencing a divorce that was devastating to my family (me and my sons). My first impression of Deborah was that I thought she was an educated suburban woman. The first time you meet a person, you usually can't tell what that person has been through in their life because the outcome looks so good. As Christians, we are supposed to support and help one another. I had no idea that my help would come from a woman who had a background so different than my own. What I found amazing is that although Deborah had not been mothered and had come from a highly dysfunctional background with no Christian experience, God used her to help me put my life back together. She not only mothered me, but my children as well. She was not brought up in the Word, but she always had a timely word for my season.

If I can be selfish for a moment, I would say that God saved Deborah to use her to save me, and I appreciate him for that. I never knew how difficult divorce could be on a family, especially children, but God used the gifts, talents and anointing of this great woman of God to rescue this dying person. Deborah has walked alongside me throughout my healing, and now I am able to minister healing to others. Deborah has mentored me in ministry, and it's extraordinary to see God use her on the streets to minister to so many lost and hopeless people. In the short time I've known them, I've witnessed Deborah and JohnRoss Ministries bless thousands of people.

Minister Leila Newman
"Glorious Life Worship Center"
Hazelcrest, Illinois

Marriage Renewal

I (Tracey Brim) remember a time when I was being challenged in my marriage. I called Deborah to announce that I had truly had enough and my mind was made up about leaving my husband. She listened attentively (prayerfully, I'm sure). When I finished talking, Deborah quietly but firmly reminded me that I could not quit or give up on my marriage. She said, "We are a covenant people and marriage is a God-ordained covenant."

She encouraged me to seek the face of God about what I thought was wrong in this distressing situation. She offered up a prayer of faith for me, and I am still married today! My husband and I have been married for 21 years. God has given us a gift for marriage ministry and we have taught many enrichment classes to married couples. I have specifically been in ministry for twenty-plus years and have been born-again for more than twenty-five years.

I was raised in the church and, after all these years of exposure to Christianity, I am not easily impressed with people or words, but the genuine anointing on Deborah Ross's life for marriage, evangelism and women is phenomenal. There are few people I seek out personally for counsel because I am a pastor, but whenever I have come to her for wisdom, I am always pointed back to Jesus.

In the summer of 2004, JohnRoss Ministries did an outreach for our church, Work of His Hands Ministries. The church is located on the west side of Chicago in a high-crime, drug-infested area. We were abundantly blessed by the God-given anointing of this ministry team that included Deborah and Maurice's daughters. As a result of their evangelistic effort, many souls came to the Lord. Backsliders recommitted and our own church experienced a renewal of excitement for evangelism.

One aspect I personally find unique is the fact that Deborah Ross's service in ministry is not one-dimensional. She is adamant about the importance of ministry to the family. She is passionate about evangelism. She has a special commitment to racial reconciliation, particularly among the women of God. Her diversity in ministry has proven to be a great asset in my life.

Pastor Tracey Brim
"Work of His Hands Ministry"
Chicago, Illinois

Working All Things Together for Glory and for Good

We do not know all of the reasons that God permits certain things to occur in our lives. I believe that God has purposes for all that He allows, but some of those purposes we will not understand until we get to heaven. However, the Bible teaches that sometimes God is pruning so that we may become fruitful. (John 15:1-2) Sometimes God is purifying so that we may become more like Jesus. (Malachi 3:3) Sometimes God is proving or testing us in order to develop and/or to disclose us. (Genesis 22:1; Exodus 15:25; Deuteronomy 8:1-5) Sometimes God is preparing us for service. (1 Peter 5:10) God has prepared Deborah for service.

I believe that Deborah Ross is an illustration of Romans 8:28, "And we know that all things work together for good to those who love God, to those who are the called according to His purpose." God is able to take what the Devil means for evil and to work it together for His glory and for the good of those who love Him and who are the called according to his purpose. (Genesis 50:20; cf. John 10:10)

During the time that Deborah was a member of the church that I pastor, I was impressed with her concern for lost souls. Deborah has the gift of an evangelist. God has prepared Deborah for the ministry in which she is now involved, and He did it all for His glory.

Pastor-Teacher, Julius R. Malone
"New Testament Church"
Milwaukee, Wisconsin

A Church in the City

A few years ago, shortly after the first screening of the movie "Titanic," a young couple from the suburbs decided to leave Eastbrook for more comfortable and safer ground. However, they hesitated for one Sunday because God had spoken to them from the ending of the movie. On the way home, the wife had told her husband that now she understood the vision of Eastbrook. Eastbrook was like the full lifeboats of the sinking Titanic that turned around and went back to rescue more drowning passengers. Most of the lifeboats did not go back. The insight was compelling, but the couple left for the suburbs anyway. In a sense, this dear couple represents much of the church that knows better than it lives.

People are indeed drowning in the city. If truth were known, they are drowning in the outer city as well. Maurice and Deborah are among those who have returned to the city they could have escaped for good. Their appearance among us was a great encouragement to us all. They were streetwise, but also street-prepared. Their family, team and trailer were designed to bring hope to the most devastated areas.

I remember when an especially heinous crime was committed at 21st and Brown in Milwaukee. The next Sunday, Deborah and Maurice led the church down to 21st and Brown to minister to the people of the area.

I can still see some of our members from the suburbs, Elm Grove, Grafton, Mequon, Whitefish Bay and the like standing in the street next to their city counterparts, praising God and listening to Deborah and Maurice preach the life-changing love of Jesus to all who were present.

The JohnRoss Ministries has continued to expand and now, like the church, is multi-ethnic in makeup. The appearance of Hispanic brothers and sisters on the team has added extra impact in our badly divided city. This is characteristic of the Ross family in general as they continue to grow and develop their gifts and vision to include more people. At present, they teach evangelism to the church in our spiritual formation classes, with a unique dimension of leading interested students into our neighborhood for door-to-door prayer evangelism.

Deborah and Maurice are an encouragement to me personally and are a rich resource to help me understand our great city and its precious people. And of course we could talk of the great Woman to Woman ministry Deborah leads, which draws women together and has expanded into the Chicago area. Deborah is an intense Spirit-filled visionary that we are committed to rejoice in for years to come.

Pastor Marc Erickson
Eastbrook Church
Milwaukee, Wisconsin

About the Author

Deborah Ann Ross is a native Chicagoan. She received Jesus Christ in 1981. Her salvation in Christ has brought her much healing, deliverance and victory over sin. As a result of knowing Jesus, her favorite thing to do is to introduce others to Him. She is married to Maurice Ross and is the mother of five children. Fifteen years were dedicated to homeschooling their children. She is the manager for her daughters' string quartet, "Sisters of PraiZe." Deborah and her husband serve as Pastors of Evangelism at their church. Her passionate topics are raising a Godly seed, evangelism, and racial reconciliation. She is an active speaker, as well as the founder and executive director of Woman to Woman Retreats, which is a ministry for racial and denominational reconciliation. She is the visionary and co-founder of JohnRoss Ministries' "Church on Wheels."

ABOUT THE AUTHOR

Her family serves as missionaries to cities across America.

BACK ON THE STREETS

Cover design

Photo layouts

by

Maurice Ross

Deborah 12 years old with the neighbors children.

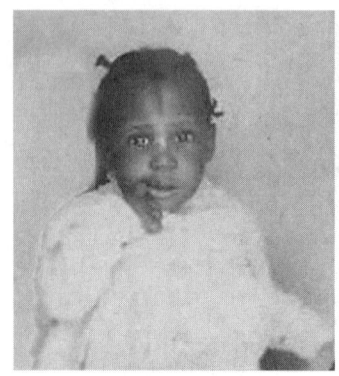
1 year old

8 years old

13 years old

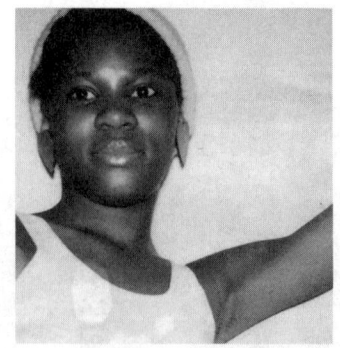
14 years old

Ricky and Deborah

Little Ricky and Deborah

Numbing the pain

Newly weds

A new marriage and added blessings!

5 year vow renewal

The homeschooling years

Sisters of PraiZe

Praise Him on the strings

Praise Him in the dance

Compelling them to come in

The Church on Wheels

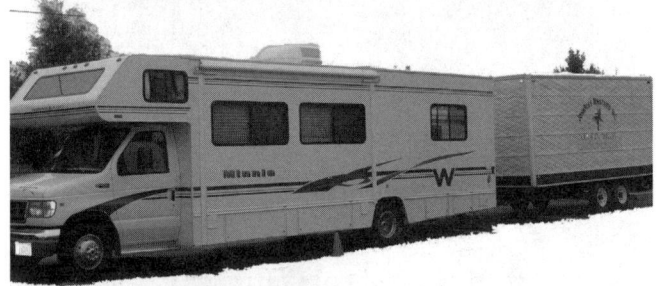

Easter Outreach

Back-To-School Outreach

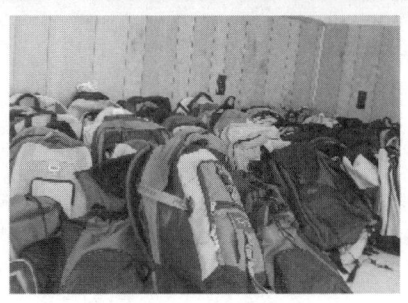

Thanksgiving Outreach

Christmas Outreach

Contact Information

JohnRoss Ministries

P.O. Box 18075

Milwaukee, WI 53218

www.jrministries.org

JohnRoss Ministries is a tax exempt 501(c)3 non-profit

organization.

All contributions are tax-deductible.